Twisted Mary 3
The Beginning of The End

Twisted Mary 3
The Beginning of The End

BY

TRACY WILSON

Http://beautifulpublications.com

Published by
Beautiful Publications LLC
Stratford, CT 06614

PRINT ISBN: 978-1-7334002-6-8
EBOOK ISBN: 978-1-7334002-7-5

Printed in the United States of America

Dedication

I dedicate this series to all the women that were given second chances and smart enough to take them.

Chapter 1

"Theresa! How are you?" the receptionist asked as they walked in...

"I'm good..." Theresa answered...

"I see you brought a friend..."

"Yes I did – this is Starr..." she said as she introduced her...

"Nice to meet you Starr..."

"Thank you – and this is my husband, Chandler..."

"Nice meeting you Chandler – I'm Shelly..."

"Nice to meet you Shelly..." Chandler said...

"Are you here to see the doctor Starr?" Shelly asked...

"Yes I am..." she beamed...

"Is this your first time here?"

"Yes it is..."

"Okay – I need you to give me your insurance card and fill out these forms..." she said as she gave Starr a clipboard with 10 sheets full of questions...

"Oh my God – I have to fill out all these?" Starr laughed...

"I'm afraid so..." Shelly answered...

"Here's her insurance card..." Chandler said as he pulled the card out his wallet and handed it to Shelly...

"Oh my God – Chandler!" Starr laughed as she pointed to the questions...

"What the hell?" Chandler exclaimed...

"I know – right?" she laughed...

"That's funny – we usually get an angry reaction..." Shelly said...

"Oh boy – the questions..." Theresa said...

"Yes!" Chandler and Starr said in unison...

"Do people actually answer these?" Starr asked...

"Sometimes..." Shelly answered...

"They're so personal!" Starr said...

"You don't have to answer anything you don't want to..." Shelly said...

"I'm not – don't worry!" Starr laughed...

"Hello Theresa..." Dr. Russo said as she came out into the waiting area...

"Hi LuAnn..." Theresa said...

"Are you here to see me today?"

"Yes I am – and I brought my friend to see you too..." she answered as she pointed to Starr...

"Hello – I'm Dr. LuAnn Russo – but you can call me LuAnn..."

"Hi LuAnn – I'm Starr – and this is my husband, Chandler..."

"Nice to meet you Starr, nice to meet you Chandler – so – who's going first?"

"Theresa is!" Starr exclaimed...

"I guess I'm going first..." Theresa laughed as she got up and followed LuAnn into the examination room...

"How's everything going?" LuAnn asked...

"Things are going good..." Theresa sighed...

"I take it that means you're trying again?"

"I wouldn't exactly say that..." she answered as the got undressed, put on the gown, and got up on the table...

"Any tenderness?" LuAnn asked as she examined Theresa's breasts...

"A little..."

"When was your last period?"

"Last month..."

"Hmmm... okay... scoot down here so I can see what's going on..."

"Okay..."

"Hmm... everything seems to be okay... and pain when I push here?"

"A little..."

"Hmmm... Theresa – did you give us a urine sample?"

"No..."

"Here – give me a sample – use the bathroom over there..." LuAnn said as she pointed to the bathroom...

"Okay..." Theresa said as she got down from the table, peed in the cup, and called LuAnn... "LuAnn – I'm done..."

"Okay – I'ma take this – you wait here..." she said as she took the sample and went out to the lobby... "Shelly – I need you to call Theresa's husband – tell him he needs to get here asap..."

"Okay..." Shelly said as she called Charles... "Dr. Russo needs to see you right away... I don't know... okay..."

"Chandler – did you hear that?" Starr whispered...

"What?"

"The doctor told Shelly to call Charles...

"Okay..."

"I hope she's okay..."

"I'm sure she's fine..."

"Where is she?" Charles asked as he came in...

"I'll get the doctor for you..." Shelly answered as she called LuAnn... "Charles is here... uh huh... okay..."

"Charles – come with me..." LuAnn said as Charles followed her down the hall...

"Charles – you're here!" Theresa exclaimed as he came into the room...

"Yes... I'm here..." he said as he took her hand...

"LuAnn – what's wrong?" Theresa asked...

"I need you to get up on the table so I can do a sonogram..." LuAnn answered...

"Okay…"

"This is gonna be cold…" she said as she put the jelly on Theresa's belly and turned on the machine…

"Congratulations… you're pregnant…"

"Oh my God! Charles… we're pregnant…"

"We're pregnant…" Charles whispered as he squeezed Theresa's hand and kissed her…

"Here's your baby's first picture…" LuAnn said as she handed Charles two prints of the sonogram…

"We're gonna have a baby…" Charles whispered as tears rolled down his face…

"We're really having a baby?" Theresa asked as she got up off the table…

"Yes… We're having a baby… see?" Charles answered as he showed her the sonogram…

"Oh Charles… I love you…"

"I love you too…" he said as he pulled Theresa into a kiss. When they went back out into the waiting area they were all smiles…

"Theresa – are you okay?" Starr asked…

"We're pregnant…" they both answered in unison…

"Aww… I'm so happy for y'all…" Starr said as she got up, hugged Theresa, and they held each other while crying…

"Congratulations…" Chandler said as he got up to hug Charles…

"I love you man…" Charles said as he hugged Chandler and cried…

"Ummm… okay…" Chandler said…

"If it wasn't for you – we'd be divorced…" Charles said…

"God works in mysterious ways…" Chandler said…

"He sure does…" Charles agreed…

"Alright ladies – break it up – Starr – Chandler – come with me…" LuAnn said as they followed her into the examination room…

"Good morning!" Vanessa beamed as she walked into the dining room…

"Good morning Vanessa – are we behind schedule?" Wayne asked…

"Not at all – it's just 8 now…" she answered…

"Good morning Vanessa – I can't wait to get our keys!" I exclaimed…

"I'm happy to help you get outta this hotel as soon as possible – shall we go now?" she asked…

"Let's go!" I exclaimed as I got up along with Wayne and we followed her out to the parking lot, got in her car, and headed to her office…

"Chandler – you sit here – Starr – I need you to take everything off, put this gown on with the opening to the front, and sit on the table – I'll be right back…" LuAnn said and then she went to leave the room…

"Where are you going?" Starr asked…

"I'm giving you privacy…"

"Aren't you going to see me naked anyway?"

"Yes…"

"Well you might as well stay…" Starr laughed…

"If you'd rather I stay – I'll stay – but I need to go get your papers – get undressed – I'll be right back…" she said as she left the room…

"Here Chandler – hold my clothes…"

"Okay…"

"Chandler – why are you looking at me like that?" Starr asked as she put on the gown and got up on the table…

"I can't look at you?"

"Not like that…"

"Like what?"

"Like you want to make love to me…" she answered as LuAnn knocked on the door…

"Come in…" Starr said…

"Starr – we need to talk…"

"Okay…"

"You didn't answer a lot of the questions…"

"I don't think you need to know all my business!" Starr laughed…

"Starr – I don't care how many partners you've had – I don't care about oral sex – I don't care about anal sex – you're right – that's not my business – but I am concerned about the other questions…"

"What other questions?"

"Why haven't you had a pap smear?"

"I just never had one…"

"Starr – annual pap smears are important – especially among young black women – it's your best chance at preventing cervical cancer and HPV…"

"I know…"

"So why haven't you had one?"

"Well…"

"Chandler – can you give us a minute?"

"Starr – you want me to stay?"

"I want Chandler to stay…"

"Starr – you know you can trust me – right?"

"I guess…"

"Why did you come here today?"

"Because I'm pregnant…"

"You're pregnant? How do you know you're pregnant?"

"I took a pregnancy test at home…"

"Congratulations…"

"Thank you…" Chandler said…

"Starr – I need to ask you a personal question…

"Okay…"

"Chandler was your first – right?"

"Yea…" Starr answered as she put her head down…

"Starr... you don't need to be embarrassed..."

"I don't?"

"No... you don't..." LuAnn answered as she took Starr's hand...

"Okay..."

"Now that I know – I'm actually relieved..."

"You are?"

"Yes – I have a lot of patients that have multiple partners, don't use protection, don't get checked, and come see me only after they catch something..."

"Oh wow..."

"Okay Starr – we're going to do a couple of things – first – I need to take some blood..."

"Why?"

"We need to know your blood type – if you're positive – it's not an issue – if you're negative – we need to monitor you closely – and you'll need a shot to protect you and your baby if you want more children..."

"I don't understand..."

"Okay – your immune system contains protective substance called antibodies that fight off bacteria or any material that your immune system doesn't recognize...

"Okay..."

"Antibodies also attack antigens that aren't present in your natural blood type – so if your blood is positive – you're okay – if your blood type is RH Negative and your baby is positive – your immune system will make antibodies against your baby's red blood cells...

"Oh wow..."

"If that happens then your baby could be born with jaundice – that's a yellowing of the skin and whites of the eyes, lethargy, or low muscle tone..."

"Can you protect my baby?"

"Yes – that's why I'm taking your blood. It takes time – that doesn't happen overnight and it doesn't happen often – but it does happen..."

"It is possible I could have a miscarriage?"

"That has happened..."

"Oh no..."

"Starr – I'm not saying if you're negative you'll automatically miscarry – I'm just saying it has happened..."

"Okay..."

"Do you know what your mother's blood type is?"

"No..."

"What about your father?"

"No..."

"Okay – I'm going to take some blood – we'll send it over and find out what your blood type is – and we'll take it from there – okay?"

"Okay..."

"Chandler – do you know what your blood type is?"

"I'm AB Negative..."

"Okay – I'll note that in your wife's chart..." she said as she prepared the needle and tubes... "Are you ready Starr?"

"I'm ready..."

"Okay – hold still – it'll just be a pinch..." she said as she inserted the needle and took Starr's blood... "Okay – we'll get this out to the lab – now I need to do a breast exam – lie down on your back..."

"Okay..."

"Have you ever done a self-breast exam?"

"No..."

"Well – when you come for your annual checkup, the breast exam is part of that..."

"Okay..."

"Any tenderness?" she asked as she examined Starr's breasts...

"A little..."

"Everything seems fine – now – I need you to scoot down to the bottom of the table and open your legs...

"Okay..."

"Since you've never had a pap smear – I'm going to give you one..."

"But I'm already pregnant..."

"Yes I know – but we're going to use this first one to compare to each one you get afterwards..."

"Okay..."

"If you feel any discomfort – let me know..."

"Okay…"

"I'm going to insert the speculum into your vagina – it's going to hold your vagina open so I can see your cervix – then I'll do your pap smear – then we'll take it out…"

"Does it hurt?"

"No…"

"Can I see it?"

"Sure…" she answered as she held up the plastic speculum…

"That doesn't look so bad…"

"It's not – it might be a little uncomfortable though…"

"Okay…"

"Are you ready?"

"I'm ready…"

"Okay – here goes – try to relax…"

"Okay…"

"Alright – it's in – I'm going to open it now – you okay?"

"I'm okay…"

"Hmmm… Chandler – come take a look…"

"Okay…" Chandler said as he got up and went to look between Starr's legs…

"That's the cervix…"

"Oh… okay…"

"I'm going to take this swab, get a sample, and then we'll send it to the lab…"

"Okay…" Chandler said…

"How you doing Starr?"

"I'm okay…"

"Okay – I'm swabbing the cervix now – you okay?"

"I'm okay..."

"Okay – I'm done – I'm going to take the speculum out now..."

"Okay..."

"Now I'm going to check your ovaries and your fallopian tubes – I'm going to put on a glove, put some jelly on the glove, and stick my fingers in your vagina..."

"Why?"

"I need to check the position of your cervix and I can only do that with my hand..."

"Okay..."

"Here I go – you okay?"

"I'm okay..."

"Any tenderness when I push here?"

"A little..."

"How 'bout here?"

"A little..."

"Okay – now for the best part..."

"The best part?"

"Yes – I'm going to do a sonogram and see how pregnant you are..." she answered as she squirted jelly on Starr's stomach...

"That's cold!"

"Sorry about that..." she said as she smoothed it on Starr's stomach and turned on the machine... "Oh my goodness..."

"Is something wrong?" Chandler asked...

"Look at the screen..." she answered...

"Oh my God – is that two babies?" Chandler asked...

"That's two babies..." she answered...

"We're having twins..." Chandler whispered as he took Starr's hand and started to cry...

"I love you Chandler..."

"I love you too..." he said as he leaned over to kiss her...

"I'll print these pictures for you..." LuAnn said as she printed the sonogram for them and let them have their moment... "Here you go..." she said as she handed them to Chandler...

"Thank you LuAnn..." he sniffed as he put the pictures in his pocket...

"Okay Starr – you can sit up now – but I have a couple of questions I need to ask..."

"Okay..."

"How's your appetite?"

"I don't eat like I should..."

"I'm starting you on prenatal vitamins – I need you to take them every day – understand?"

"Yes Maam..."

"Okay – any fatigue?"

"Yes – I'm always tired..."

"Chandler – keep an eye on her – and make sure she gets plenty of rest..."

"Yes Maam..." Chandler acknowledged...

"Any fainting?"

"Yea..."

"How often?"

"One time…"

"That's one time too many – I need to see you again in two weeks…"

"Okay…"

"You're about two and a half months – about 10 weeks – you should have your babies the first week in January…"

"I don't think I'll make it to January…"

"Why not?"

"Because I was born at 8 months and so was my brother…"

"I see – well – we'll be keeping an eye on you so we'll know when you get closer – now – here's what you need to do…"

"Yes LuAnn?"

"You need to eat, you need to take your prenatal vitamins, you need to rest, and you need to see me in two weeks – got it?"

"Got it…"

"Okay – you can get dressed – here's the prescription for the prenatal vitamins – I'll see you in two weeks – congratulations again…" she said as she left the room…

"Chandler…" Starr whispered as she started to cry and Chandler grabbed her into a hug…

"I know…" he whispered as he moved her hair out of her face and cried with her…

"I'm so happy…"

"Me too…"

"I need to call Mommy…"

"Okay – but let's do it outside…"

"About time!" Theresa said as they walked back into the waiting area…

"Shelly?"

"Yes Starr?"

"I need to make another appointment for two weeks from today…"

"Okay – how's 9 a.m.?"

"That's fine…" Starr sighed…

"Is everything okay?" Theresa asked…

"We're having twins…" Starr beamed…

"Oh my God!" Theresa screamed as she jumped up to hug Starr and they started crying…

"Congratulations man!" Charles said as he got up and grabbed Chandler into a hug…

"Thank ya, thank ya!" Chandler said…

"Chandler – give me the pictures…" Starr said…

"Okay – here…" he said as he handed her the pictures. Starr took a picture of the sonograms with her cellphone, sent them to her mother, and then she gave the pictures back to Chandler…

"Starr's not cooking tonight…" Chandler said…

"Aww man!" Charles exclaimed…

"Ain't nobody cookin' tonight – we goin' to Testos – my treat!"

"Okay!" they all said in unison as they left the doctor's office…

Chapter 2

"Wayne – we're here!" I exclaimed as Vanessa parked the car...

"I see..." Wayne laughed...

"Let's go inside..." Vanessa said as we got out the car...

"I'm so excited!" I exclaimed...

"I'm glad you're so happy..." Wayne said...

"The Robinson's are here – is Mr. Baisden here?" Vanessa asked...

"He's inside already..." the receptionist answered...

"Okay – come with me..." Vanessa said as she took us in the room... "Good morning Mr. Baisden – these are my clients, Mr. and Mrs. Robinson..."

"Nice to meet you both – congratulations – and thank you..." he said as he shook our hands...

"Thank you – and you're welcome..." Wayne said...

"Okay – here's all the papers you need to sign – they've already been signed by Mr. Baisden..." Vanessa said...

"Okay Mrs. Robinson – are you ready?"

"I'm ready!" I exclaimed...

"Okay – pen please..." Wayne said as Vanessa handed him the pile of papers. Wayne started signing the papers and passed them over to me as he signed them. I signed them and passed them to Vanessa. This took about 30 minutes as we stopped to read over each disclosure form, title search, inspection, etc...

"Congratulations – here's your keys – wait here – I'm going to make you a copy of these papers and then you can go home..." Vanessa said as she handed the keys to Wayne...

"Congratulations – I need to get going – thanks again..." Mr. Baisden said as he got up to leave...

"Thank you – bye!" I exclaimed...

"Here you go – it's been a pleasure working with you both..." Vanessa said as she handed me the envelope..."

"Same here..." I said as we hugged...

"Thank you Vanessa..." Wayne said as they hugged...

"You're welcome – can I take you somewhere?"

"You can take us back to the hotel..." Wayne answered...

"Okay – let's go..." she said as we followed her out to the car and got in...

"I won't be able to stay – I have another closing this afternoon..."

"That's fine Vanessa..." Wayne said. When we got to the hotel I couldn't wait to get out the car...

"I can't wait to go home!" I exclaimed...

"Thank you Vanessa..." Wayne said as he got out...

"You're welcome – have a good day!" she said as she drove off...

"Let's check out now..." I said...

"Mary..."

"Yes Wayne?"

"Wait a minute..."

"Okay..."

"Come back to the room with me..."

"Okay..." I sighed. When we got upstairs, Wayne could tell I was disappointed...

"I have a surprise for you..."

"Okay..."

"It'll be worth it – I promise..." he said as he pulled me into a kiss...

"Okay..." I sighed as we went back downstairs to the lobby, went out to the car, and got in. Wayne started the car and took off while I checked my message... "Oh my God!" I exclaimed...

"What?" Wayne asked...

"They're having twins!"

"Starr?"

"Yes! See?" I said as I showed him the pictures...

"Oh wow..."

"Hi Mommy!"

"Starr! Congratulations! I'm so happy for you!"

"Thank you Mommy!"

"We got the keys!"

"You did?"

"We did kid…" Wayne answered…

"Congratulations…" Chandler said…

"Thank you Chandler…"

"Mommy – the doctor had a lot of questions…"

"Like what?" I asked…

"Mommy – what's your blood type?"

"I'm A Positive…"

"Oh…"

"Why?"

"The doctor was telling me about the risks with Negative blood types…"

"That's your father…"

"Daddy's RH Negative?"

"Yea…"

"Am I RH Negative?"

"Yes…"

"Oh…"

"What else did she ask you?"

"Oh you know… the usual stuff they ask…"

"Okay – we're on the highway – the call may drop – we'll call you later – okay?"

"Okay Mommy – love you – love you Dad…"

"Love you too..." we said in unison as I hung up...

"Congratulations Grandpa..." I laughed...

"Congratulations Grandma..." Wayne laughed as we pulled into the parking lot...

"Oh my God! I Hop!" I exclaimed.

Chapter 3

"Beautiee?"

"Yes?"

"Where are you?"

"I'm in here…"

"In where?"

"Where else?" she laughed as Bazil came into the bathroom…

"Is that what I think it is?"

"Uh huh…" she smiled mischievously while waving the pregnancy test…

"Oh my God… you're pregnant?"

"Yes… I'm pregnant…" she whispered as she started crying…

"Beautiee…" Bazil whispered as he kissed her and started crying himself…

"Yes… My Thirst Quencher…"

"We're having another baby…" he said as he picked Beautiee up, she wrapped her legs around him, he carried her into the bedroom, and they fell back onto the bed. Bazil couldn't wait to get inside her… and he didn't…

"Bazil… Haaa…."

"Yeesss…" They barely started and Bazil heard Jay stirring… "Fuck!" he moaned as they both heard Jay but neither one wanted to stop…

"Why… does he… always… start… when… it gets… so… fuckin'… good…" Beautiee panted…

"Is it good?"

"Fuck… Yeesss…"

"Tell me…"

"It's… good…"

"You want more?"

"Yes… oh God… yes…"

"Cum for me…"

"Fuck me… yes… right there… don't stop… I'm cumming… I'm cumming… Fuuuccckkk!"

"That's it… give it to me… uuuggghhh… you're so fuckin' wet… shit… fuck… Uuuggghhhh!" Bazil collapsed on top of Beautiee and she wrapped her legs around him, pulled him into a kiss, and stuck her tongue in his mouth… "Mmmm… you want more…"

"Yes… I want more…"

"Jay needs… to… eat…"

"I know…"

"I need to get up…"

"I know…"

"I need to get up…"

"I know…"

"You need to let me go…"

"Never…"

"I love you…"

"I love you more…" she said as she relaxed her legs and put them down…"

"I'll make it up to you later…" he said as he got up and went to get Jay…

"Good morning…" Beautiee beamed as she took Jay in her arms and took her breast out to feed him. Jay latched on and sucked to his hearts' content as they talked…

"I can't believe we're having another baby…" Bazil said…

"What?" Jay said as he spit Beautiee's breast out his mouth…

"What's wrong Jay? You full already?" Beautiee asked as she tried to put her breast back in his mouth and he wouldn't take it… "Hmmm… not that hungry I guess…"

"That's odd – he usually eats for about 20 to 30 minutes…" Bazil said…

"You okay Jay?" Beautiee asked as she picked Jay up and looked him in his face…

"No… I'm the baby!" he said…

"I wonder what he's saying?" Bazil asked…

"What are you saying Jay?" Beautiee asked as she held him and kissed him but Jay squirmed to get away from her…

"Hmmm… let me take him…" Bazil said as he took Jay from her… "What's going on Jay?" Bazil asked as Jay squirmed to get away from him… "Stop it!" Bazil boomed. Jay's eyes got really big, his lips trembled, and then he let out a scream...

"Waaaaaah!"

"You gon' make me put you back in your room..." Bazil said. Jay calmed down, stopped squirming and laid his head on Bazil's chest... "I love you too..."

"You do?" Jay asked...

"He's really talkin' to us..." Beautiee said...

"I wish I knew what he was saying..."

"Me too..." Beautiee said as she got up to take Jay from Bazil... "Jay – you need to finish eating so you can be strong enough to help me take care of your lil' brother..." she said as she sat on the bed, took her breast out, and put it in Jay's mouth...

"I'm gonna have a lil' brother?" Jay asked with Beautiee's breast in his mouth...

"Jay..." Beautiee laughed... "Stop playing and eat!"

"Okay Mommy... I'll eat..." Jay said as he started sucking...

"Damn I wish we knew what he was saying!" Bazil laughed...

"Me too – but at least he's eating..."

"So are we going to see Dr. Julianne?"

"No – we're going to see Dr. Kourounis..."

"Who's that?"

"She's an OB/GYN here in Milford..."

"Oh... okay..."

"Alright Jay – you need to go back to your room so we can take a shower and get dressed – then we're going out okay?"

"Okay Mommy..." Jay cooed...

"I'ma start recording him..." Bazil laughed...

"Keisha!"

"What?" Troy got up out the bed, went into the bathroom, and pushed up on Keisha...

"Who you talkin' to like that?" he asked as he pulled her into his arms and kissed her...

"You..." she laughed...

"Whatchu hiddin' behind your back..." Troy asked as he snatched the pregnancy test out her hand... "Keisha... you're pregnant?"

"Yes..." she answered as she shook her head...

"We're having a baby?"

"Yes..." she answered as she shook her head again and started to cry...

"I... love... you..." Troy said as he kissed her and started crying...

"I... love... you... too..." she said as she wrapped her arms around his neck, wrapped her legs around his waist, and he carried her into the bedroom...

"Okay Jay – let's get you dressed..." Beautiee said as she picked Jay up out his crib...

"Good thing we have room for another crib..." Bazil said...

"I can't wait to go shopping for another crib..." Beautiee said as she dressed Jay...

"You mean you can't wait to sit down in front of the computer and have furniture delivered..." Bazil laughed...

"Another crib? What's a crib?" Jay asked...

"There he goes again..." Bazil said...

"Jay – we're going to the doctor – and then we're going to make room in here for your lil' brother..." Beautiee said as she picked him up...

"My lil' brother is moving in here? With me?" Jay asked...

"Oh my goodness – he's excited!" Bazil laughed as he took Jay and held him...

"What if we're having a girl?" Beautiee asked...

"Then we'll need to give her her own room..."

"No – my lil' sister needs to be with me so I can protect her!" Jay said as he squirmed...

"Jay – you sure have a lot to tell us huh?" Bazil laughed...

"I wish I knew what he was saying..." Beautiee said...

"Maybe we can look online for a baby language translator..." Bazil laughed as they went downstairs and went out the door...

"Hello Keisha, hello Troy – what brings you in today – you're not due for an annual until the end of the year…" Kay said…

"Dr. Kourounis – we're pregnant!" Keisha beamed…

"Oh my goodness – congratulations! I didn't think you were ever gonna have children!"

"Thank you doctor…" Troy said…

"Please – call me Kay…"

"Thank you Kay…" Troy said…

"Thank you Kay…" Keisha beamed…

"When did you find out you were pregnant?"

"This morning…" Troy answered…

"Oh wow – okay – Keisha – you know the drill…"

"Yea – I know the drill…" she laughed as she started getting undressed…

"Keisha – wait a minute!" Kay laughed…

"Why? You 'bout to see it all anyway…" Keisha laughed as she took off her clothes, took a gown out the bag, put it on, and jumped up on the table…

"You're right…" Kay laughed… "So did you give us a urine sample?"

"Yes Kay…"

"Good – I'ma take some blood…"

"Aww damn! Why?"

"Keisha – you might as well get used to needles – especially now that you're pregnant…" she said as she took blood from Keisha's arm and put the tubes to the side... "Okay – scoot on down..."

"Alright... hold on a minute..." Keisha said as she scooted down on the table...

"Any problems?" Kay asked as she examined Keisha...

"Nope..."

"When was your last period?"

"Last month..."

"Any tenderness when I push here?"

"Nope..."

"Okay – you can get up – I'll call you when I get your blood work – come back and see me in a month...

"That's it?" Troy asked...

"That's if for now – her urine test is positive – you're not having any problems – keep it up!" Kay said as she patted Troy on his back...

"Keisha – Kay just told me to keep it up – you know what that means..." he said as he smiled at her mischievously...

"Hell yea!" Keisha said as she got dressed...

"Congratulations again – I'll see you next month..." Kay said as she left the examining room...

"C'mere..." Troy said as he pulled Keisha into a kiss..."

"Don't start that shit in here Troy..." Keisha laughed...

"I'll start…" he said as he kissed her neck… "Anywhere…" he said as he kissed her between her breasts… "I want to…" he breathed as he kissed her again…

"I know that's right…" she breathed as she kissed him back…

"Excuse me – is someone in here?" Beautiee asked as she knocked on the door…

"Beautiee?" Keisha asked as she snatched the door open…

"Keisha?" Beautiee asked…

"Whatchall doin' here?" they both said in unison…

"Oh my God!" they both yelled as they hugged each other crying…

"Congratulations!" Beautiee said as she wiped her eyes…

"You too!"

"I'm so happy for y'all!"

"Me too!"

"Congratulations Troy…" Bazil said as they hugged…

"You too…" Troy said…

"Hey Jay – you know you gonna have a lil' brother or sister – right?" Keisha asked as she took Jay from Bazil…

"I know – Mommy and Daddy told me!" Jay cooed…

"Troy – you hear him talkin'?" Keisha laughed…

"I hear him…" Troy laughed as Kay came back into the room…

"Oh my goodness – hello Mr. Osgood!" she beamed…

"Hello doctor…" Bazil said…

"This must be your wife…" she said as she looked at Beautiee…

"This is my wife…"

"Beautiee – it's so nice to meet you…"

"Thank you doctor…" Beautiee said…

"My name is Kayvonne – but all my patients call me Kay…"

"Nice to meet you Kay…"

"I guess congratulations are in order?"

"Yes Kay…" Beautiee sighed…

"Congratulations – we need to talk…"

"Oh shit – Beautiee you in trouble…" Keisha said as she gave Jay back to Bazil and left the room with Troy…

"Something wrong doctor?" Bazil asked…

"Hmmm… let's see – your wife hasn't had a pap smear since…" she answered as she flipped through the papers… "since before she had the baby…"

"His name is Jay…" Bazil interrupted…

"Hello Jay – nice to meet you – now – where was I – oh – that's right – your baby was delivered in Boston – which is fine – but not by your doctor…"

"My last doctor doesn't deliver babies…" Beautiee interrupted…

"Exactly – you didn't follow up and get prenatal care – and your baby was born early – why?"

"Well... to be honest... I went to Dr. Julianne because I trust her..."

"Okay – so why didn't you come see me sooner?"

"I've been through a lot in the last year – I planned on coming to see you after the wedding – but I went into labor and... you know the rest..."

"So you saw Dr. Julianne up until you were 8 months pregnant?"

"Yes..."

"Did you take prenatal vitamins?"

"Yes..."

"Well... that's something... and... I guess you had no way of knowing your son was going to be born at 8 months..."

"No... I didn't... it wasn't the wedding night they had planned!" Beautiee laughed...

"Oh my God! Let me get some blood..." Kay said as she prepared the needle, took blood, and put the tubes to the side... "What happened?"

"We all went to bed..." Beautiee said...

"After the wedding?"

"Yea... and then I went into labor..."

"Oh wow..."

"So our daughter, her husband, and my husband's baby momma came into the room..."

"Wait..." Kay laughed... "Did you just say your husband's baby momma?"

"Yes..."

"I can't..." she laughed...

"So Bazil was holding my hand and every time a contraction hit – he'd kiss me..."

"Aww... that's sweet..."

"I didn't know what else to do..." Bazil laughed...

"You held her hand and kissed her – that's pretty much what all husbands do until the contractions get so bad they get kicked out the room..." Kay laughed...

"So Mary – his baby momma – got on the bed and started rubbing my back – Starr – our daughter – got the phone and started recording – Chandler – her husband – turned his back to us – and Bazil delivered our son after I started pushing..."

"You delivered your son?" Kay asked...

"I did..." Bazil beamed...

"And your baby momma helped your wife?"

"That's right..."

"Wow..."

"So the owner of the bed and breakfast came running upstairs to tell us people were complaining about the noise... and then he saw our son..." Beautiee said...

"Oh my God!"

"They called an ambulance for us and we went to the hospital..."

"Everything was alright?"

"Everything was fine..." Bazil answered...

"So... you're pregnant... right?"

"Yes..." Beautiee answered...

"So... you didn't wait..." Kay laughed...

"Nope..."

"Have you had any pain?"

"Nope..."

"Are you breast-feeding?"

"Yup..."

"Okay – I'm going to do an exam – I need you to take everything off and put the gown on – okay?"

"Okay Kay..." Beautiee said as she started taking off her clothes...

"Beautiee! Wait a minute!"

"Why? You gonna see everything anyway..." Beautiee laughed and then Kay started laughing...

"What's so funny?" Bazil asked...

"That's the same thing Keisha said..." she laughed as Beautiee put the gown on and got up on the table...

"Okay – scoot on down..." Kay said...

"Uh huh..." Kay said as she examined Beautiee...

"Everything okay?" Bazil asked...

"Everything looks good..." Kay answered...

"Thank you Kay..." they both said in unison...

"You're welcome – get dressed…" Kay laughed… "I'll be right back…" she said as she left the room…

"Next year we'll have two boys…" Beautiee said as she sat up, got down off the table, and started getting dressed…

"We could have a boy and a girl…" Bazil said…

"That would be two girls…"

"Starr, her little sister, her little brother, and her twins…" Bazil sighed…

"I wonder how she's doing…" Beautiee said…

"I'm sure she'll call us soon…"

"I can't wait to tell her we're gonna be pregnant together…"

"C'mere Mrs. Osgood…" Bazil said as he pulled Beautiee into a kiss…

"Mmmm… I love you…"

"I love you too…"

"I love you Mommy, I love you Daddy…" Jay cooed…

"Aww… we love you too Jay…" they said in unison as Kay walked back into the room…

"Okay Mrs. Osgood…"

"Please call me Beautiee…" Beautiee interrupted…

"Okay Beautiee – please fill this prescription for prenatal vitamins – take them every day – I'll see you next month…

"Okay – thank you Kay…" Beautiee said…

"You're welcome – and congrats again…" she said as Beautiee and Bazil walked out into the waiting area…

"Y'all good?" Troy asked…

"We're good…" Beautiee sighed…

"How you like Kay?" Keisha asked…

"She's funny!" I laughed…

"Oh so you not in trouble?"

"Naa… I'm fine…"

"I'm hungry – where we goin' to eat?" Troy asked…

"Cracker Barrel…" Bazil answered…

"Good – we gon' eat this time – dammit!" Keisha laughed…

"I know that's right!" Beautiee laughed as they all left the doctor's office.

Chapter 4

"Was it worth it?" Wayne asked...

"Yes... thank you..." I answered as I kissed him...

"You're welcome..."

"Can we check out of the hotel now? Please?"

"Not yet..."

"Okay..." I sighed...

"C'mon – let's go shopping..." Wayne said...

"Shopping?"

"You said you wanted to spend the night in our new home right?"

"Yeesss...."

"Well – we're going to need a few things..."

"Okay!" I squealed as I jumped in the car and we headed down the highway... "Where are we going?"

"Target..."

"Oh! They have everything!"

"I know..." Wayne said as he smiled and squeezed my hand...

"I can't wait to go shopping – I'm gonna get dishes, pots, pans, silverware..."

"Don't forget a table..." Wayne laughed...

"I thought we were gonna wait on furniture?"

"We need a small table for the nook in the kitchen..."

"Oh – that's right – oh – I need to make sure I get a tea kettle – and a coffee pot – or Keurig – or both!" I laughed...

"We'll need to go to the grocery store for food...

"Target has food too..."

"Oh – that's right – I forgot..."

"I need to make sure we get an air mattress too..."

"Oh God – my back will be so stiff..."

"I'll get a nice one..."

"I hope so..."

"We're here..."

"You ready?"

"I'm ready!" I squealed as I got out the car and started running towards the entrance...

"Mary! Wait!" I ran until I got to the entrance, I got a shopping cart, and waited until Wayne got there...

"I thought you were going to start without me..." he laughed...

"I wouldn't do that..."

"So how are we going to do this? Am I getting a cart too?"

"Maybe you should – just in case..." I laughed...

"I have a feeling we're gonna be here for a few hours..." he laughed...

"Maybe not – I already know what I want..." I said as I went inside and Wayne followed...

"Let's look for a table first..." Wayne said...

"Okay..." We went up and down the aisle looking at small dining tables and I got frustrated quickly... "Everything says not in stores!"

"Mary – I think I found one..."

"Where?"

"Right here..." Wayne answered as he showed me his phone...

"Wayne – I don't want to wait for it to be delivered..." I sighed...

"Mary... look..." Wayne said as he gave me his phone...

'Ooohhh... same day delivery... free 4-week trial..."

"See?"

"I see..."

"Do you like the table?"

"I like the table..."

"I love how the seats go underneath..."

"Me too..."

"Order it..."

"Okay!" I squealed... "Wayne – it says we can get it by 8 p.m. – that'll give me time to cook..."

"You wanna cook? Tonight?"

"You don't want me to cook?"

"It's our anniversary…"

"I know…"

"Let me take you out to dinner…" he said as he pulled me close to him… "And then we can go home and have dessert…" he whispered in my ear…

"Okay…" I squealed as I placed the order for the urban small dining table set… "Done!"

"Good – now let's get everything else on your list…"

"Okay – you start over there – I'm going down this isle over here – I'll be right back…"

"I'll come with you…" Wayne said as he started to follow me…

"No – I mean – I'm just getting toilet papers, soap, toothbrushes, toothpaste – nothing exciting – I'll be right back…" I said as I hurried off… "Okay – where are they?" I asked out loud as I went down the medicine isle to the aspirins…

"Can I help you with anything?" the associate asked…

"Yes – I need a pregnancy test!"

"Sure – right down here…" the associate said as he pointed to the bottom shelf. I snatched one up just in time…

"There you are! You don't have much in your cart…" Wayne laughed…

"I went down the wrong isle…" I lied as I hid the pregnancy test under my pocketbook…"

"I know – the isle with the toilet paper is over there…" Wayne laughed as I followed him to the isle. We spent a good 20 minutes or so filling up his cart and then we went to the next isle… and I found it…

"Look!" I squealed when I saw it…

"Hmmm… Intex Queen Elevated Pillow Rest Air Mattress Bed with Built-in Air Pump… sounds comfortable – okay – we'll get it…" Wayne said as he tossed it in the cart…

"You're running out of room…" I laughed…

"Gee… I wonder whose fault that is!" Wayne laughed…

"Umm… mine?"

"Ya think?" he laughed as we went to the home isle and I picked out dishes, silverware, a tea kettle, a coffee pot, a Keurig, towels, washcloths, curtains, pot holders, and pots…

"Why are you putting stuff on the bottom of the cart?" he laughed…

"I need room for food…" I laughed…

"Food?"

"Follow me…" I laughed as we went to the food isle…

"Oh my God – they have everything!" he laughed…

"I know…" I said as I got breakfast food, milk, creamer, meats, etc…

"Where are we going now?" Wayne laughed…

"Follow me…" I said as we went to the dry goods isle…

"Oh wow…" he said as I filled up the cart… "Think we got enough now?" he asked…

"I think so…" I laughed as we went to the register… "Honey – why don't you go get the car and move it to the front of the store – I'll keep an eye on the carts until you get back…"

"Okay – I'll be right back…" he said as he went to get the car…

"Excuse me – I just have one item – may I cut in front of you?" I asked the young lady…

"Hell no you ain't gettin' in front of me – you think I don't see all that shit you got?" she snapped…

"Please – I just need to pay for this before my husband comes back – it's our anniversary and I want to surprise him…" I said as I showed her the pregnancy test…

"Shoot – go 'head girl!" she squealed as she let me cut in front…

"Thanks…" I said as I hurried…

"Miss – is that stuff yours too?" the cashier asked…

"Yes – but my husband's paying for that – I'm just paying for this…"

"Okay Maam…." She said as she rung it up and put it in a bag for me…

"Thanks again…" I said…

"You're welcome girl! Happy Anniversary!" she said as Wayne walked in and I put the pregnancy test in my pocketbook...

"Hey – who's your new friend?" he asked as he pulled me into a kiss...

"I'm Rhonda – girl – he is fine!"

"Thank you Rhonda – I'm Mary..." I said as Wayne blushed...

"Nice meeting you – good luck girl!" she said as she put her things up on the conveyor belt...

"Thank you Rhonda – I'm gonna need it..." I laughed. We waited in line until we could finally start putting some of our items on the conveyor belt and the cashier started ringing up the items...

"Well damn – you sure you have enough?" somebody snapped...

"I hope so – maybe I should go back and get some more... just in case..." I said sarcastically. I heard them suck their teeth but I didn't give a damn – I was going home...

"We're done!" the cashier said as she smiled...

"Thank you so much – may I see your manager?" I asked...

"Oh my God! C'mon!" that same lady snapped...

"Excuse me – this customer wants to see you..." the casher said as the manager walked towards us...

"Yes Maam?" the manager asked...

"Thank you – she's been lovely – and she hasn't complained at all – especially with all this stuff – she packed the bags and smiled – you should consider promoting her..." I said...

"I'll take that into consideration..." the manager said...

"Thank you!" the cashier said...

"You're welcome – c'mon Honey – let's go..." I said as I pushed one cart and Wayne pushed the other... and bust out laughing...

"What's so funny?" I asked...

"We forgot something!"

"Oh my God! What'd we forget?"

"We didn't get a garbage can!" he laughed...

"You're right!" I laughed as we started putting the bags in the trunk.

Chapter 5

"Welcome to Testos..." the hostess said as Chandler, Starr, Theresa, and Charles walked in...

"Thank ya, thank ya..." Chandler said...

"Table for four?" the hostess asked...

"Yes sir..." Chandler answered as they followed the hostess to a table...

"Ooohhh... it's nice here – do they do events?" Theresa asked...

"Yes..." Starr answered..."

"Let's have a joint-baby shower – we can invite your parents – my parents – your friends – my friends..."

"Easy Theresa..." Charles laughed...

"I don't have too many people to invite..." Starr said...

"Don't you have any friends?" Theresa asked...

"I have you guys..."

"That's it?"

"Well... my supervisor is pretty cool – her son went to the academy with Chandler..."

"Is that right?" Charles asked...

"Yea…" Chandler answered…

"I'm gonna invite Ms. Crystal too…" Starr said…

"Who is Ms. Crystal?" Theresa asked…

"My section 8 caseworker…"

"Wait a minute – you wanna invite your caseworker – from section 8 – to your baby shower?" Theresa laughed…

"What's so funny?"

"I'm sorry…" Theresa laughed… "I've just never heard of that…"

"She was really nice to me – and she was really happy for us when she found out we were getting married…"

"Oh wow – usually you hear how nasty they are…" Theresa said…

"Not Ms. Crystal…" Starr said…

"She was nice…" Chandler said…

"I want to meet her…" Theresa said…

"Have you had a chance to view the menu?" the waiter asked as he came over…

"We didn't get any menus…" Charles laughed…

"Oh my goodness – I'm so sorry – let me get you some menus…" the waiter said as he turned to walk away…

"No need – we'll have stuffed twin lobster tails…" Chandler said… "Unless y'all want something different…"

"Oh no – that's fine!" Charles laughed…

"Sounds good to me!" Theresa laughed…

"Okay – we have draft beer on special – would you like that or something else?" the waiter asked...

"We'll take the draft beer – she'll have a Pepsi – and she'll have a ginger ale..." Chandler answered...

"Chandler – how'd you know I wanted Pepsi?" Theresa asked...

"I remembered from last night..."

"Oh my – a man that listens – my favorite kinda man..." she laughed...

"I wanna go see Beautiee..." Starr said...

"You sure Starr? We've already had a full day and you need to go back to work tomorrow..." Chandler said...

"I know – but I still wanna go see her..."

"What about your father?"

"Oh yea – him too..." she laughed...

"Okay – we'll eat and then y'all can come with us..." Chandler said...

"You sure?" Charles asked...

"Trust me – it'll be fine – I'll call 'em and ask 'em if they're up for company..."

"Okay then..." Charles said as the waiter brought the drinks...

"I'll be right back with your food..." the waiter said...

"Le'me call 'em now..." Chandler said...

"Hey Dad – you up for company? Me, Starr, Theresa, Charles... uh huh... we're at

Testos now… We'll tell you when we get there…
okay – see you soon…"

"Your Dad's so cool…" Charles said…

"He's actually her Dad…" Chandler
laughed…

"I can't wait to see Beautiee…" Starr said
to Theresa…

"Here's your food – if you need anything
else – please let me know…" the waiter said as he
walked away…

"Oh my God – this is sooo good!" Theresa
moaned…

"Damn – you right Babe – these are
good…" Charles agreed…

"You doin' alright Starr?" Chandler
asked…

"Mmmm hmmmm!" Starr said as she ate.
When they were finished eating Chandler paid
the check and they went out to the parking lot…

"Thanks Chandler – that was delicious!"
Charles said…

"Yes it was – thank you Chandler…"
Theresa said…

"You're welcome…" Chandler said as they
got in their car, Chandler and Starr got in the
car, and they headed to see Bazil and Beautiee.

"Hey!" Bazil said when he opened the
door…

"Beautiee – they're here…"

"Hi!" Beautiee said as she ran to hug Starr…

"Hi Beautiee…"

"I missed you…"

"I missed you too… Starr said as she hugged Beautiee back…

"Hey Dad…" Chandler said as he hugged Bazil…

"Hey Chandler…" Bazil said…

"Okay – switch!" Beautiee laughed as she pulled Chandler away from Bazil to hug him…

"Hey Beautiee…" Chandler laughed…

"Hey Chandler – I'm so glad you're back…"

"Hi Daddy…" Starr said as she hugged Bazil…"

"Hi Starr – welcome home…" Bazil said…

"Nice to see you again Bazil…" Charles said…

"Hey Charles…" Bazil said as he pulled him into a hug…

"Hi Theresa…" Beautiee said as she hugged her…

"Hi Beautiee – nice to see you…"

"Come inside…" Bazil said as they followed him into the living room…

"Troy – look at him – he wants to go to Starr!" Keisha laughed…

"Jay!" Starr said as she took him from Keisha and hugged him…

"Starr! I missed you!" Jay said…

"Did you miss me?" Starr asked…

"Yes! And guess what – Mommy's having a baby!"

"Oh yea?" Starr laughed as she sat down with Jay...

"Keisha, Troy – you remember our friends Charles and Theresa from the wedding right?"

"Yes we do – hey Theresa..." Keisha said as she got up to hug Theresa...

"Hey girl..." Theresa said...

"Hey Troy..." Charles said as he went to hug Troy...

"Hey Charles..." Troy said as he hugged Charles...

"When did Jay start talking?" Starr asked...

"He's been talking here and there – but today – he hasn't stopped!" Beautiee laughed... "Your father said we should get a baby language translator..."

"That's a good idea..." Starr said...

"Well – we have news..." Chandler said...

"Everything okay with Mary and Wayne?" Bazil asked as if he didn't already know the answer...

"They closed on their house this morning..." Chandler answered...

"Oh that's nice!" Beautiee said...

"Okay – so here goes – we went to the doctor..." Chandler started to say...

"And I'm having twins!" Starr squealed...

"Yeaaaa!" Jay said...

"Oh my God! Troy - did you see that?" Keisha said...

"Hell yea I saw it – that baby knows what the hell we're talkin' about – don't you Jay?"

"Uh huh..." Jay said...

"Oh shit! He does!" Keisha laughed...

"Congratulations..." Bazil said... "I can't wait to meet my grandchildren..."

"I knew it!" Beautiee squealed...

"Congratulations y'all..." Keisha said...

"Thank ya, thank ya!" Chandler said...

"We have news too..." Beautiee said...

"You're having another baby?" Starr asked...

"Yes we are..." Bazil said as he pulled Beautiee into a kiss...

"Yeaaaa!" Jay squealed and everybody laughcd...

"Damn – he's so happy for y'all!" Keisha laughed... "Might as well tell it – we havin' a baby too..."

"Oh wow! Congratulations!" Starr said...

"Congratulations man..." Chandler said...

"Congratulations Brother..." Charles said...

"Shit – don't leave us out Charles..." Theresa laughed...

"You too?" Starr asked...

"Us too..." Charles said as he pulled Theresa into a kiss...

"Yeaaaa!" Jay squealed again...

"Aww… that is too cute – you happy for us Jay?" Theresa asked…

"Uh huh…" Jay cooed…

"Congratulations everybody…" Chandler said…

"Congratulations y'all – that's what's up…" Troy said as he got up and everybody started hugging…

"We're going to need a bigger room at Testos…" Starr said…

"Why?" Beautiee laughed…

"Because - we're having one big baby shower – for all the mothers!"

"We are?" Keisha asked…

"Yes – we are…" Starr said… and then she got quiet…

"Starr – what's wrong?" Beautiee asked…

"I was just thinking – never mind…"

"Uh uh… - what is it?"

"I wish my mother could come…"

"Why can't she?"

"You don't mind?"

"Of course not…" Beautiee said as she pulled Starr into a hug…

"Thank you Beautiee…"

"You don't have to thank me Starr…"

"Chandler – when are you going back to work?" Bazil asked, changing the subject…

"I'll probably go back tomorrow…" Chandler answered…

"How 'bout you Starr?"

"I'm going back tomorrow…" she answered…

"I don't work…" Theresa said…

"Me either girl!" Keisha said as they high-fived…

"Beautiee – have you been back to work since Jay was born?" Starr asked…

"I've been working from home a lot – but I'm about to start going back full-time – at least until I get close to delivering this one…" she answered as she rubbed her stomach…

"Who's watching Jay?" Starr asked…

"Well… his Aunty Keisha ain't working…" Beautiee laughed…

"Yeaaa!" Jay squealed…

"Aww… you like that Jay?" Troy asked…

"Uh huh…" Jay coed…

"We need to hurry up and get that baby language translator…" Bazil laughed.

Chapter 6

"Oh my God – we have so much stuff!" I exclaimed...

"You're the one that wanted to go shopping!" Wayne laughed...

"I know, I know..." I said as I started taking the food out the bags and putting it in the refrigerator...

"I'll work on putting this table and chairs together while you do that so we have something to sit on..."

"Okay..." I sighed. As happy as I was that we were home I was also anxious as hell...

"You okay Mary?" Wayne asked...

"Yes... I'm okay..."

"C'mere..." Wayne said as he came over to me, pulled me into a hug, and kissed me... "It's finally setting in – right?"

"Yea..." I sighed, relieved that he answered his own question...

"I love you..." he said as he kissed me again...

"I love you too..."

"I can't wait to try out that air mattress..."

"I sure hope we don't bust it…" I laughed…

"If we bust it…" Wane said as he kissed my neck… "We'll just fuck on the floor…"

"Oh no – I don't want rug burns!" I laughed…

"Have you ever had any?"

"No – and I'm not trying to get any!" I laughed…

"Let's hurry up and put this stuff away – I'll hurry up with this table and chairs – I still wanna take you out…"

"Okay – but that means you have to let me go…"

"Never…" he said as he kissed me again…

"I love you too – but I can't do anything unless you let me…" I laughed…

"Okay… I'll get back to this table and chairs…" Wayne said as he pulled it out of the box and layed the pieces on the floor…

"You don't need a screw driver?" I asked…

"Naa… this piece here will tighten all the screws…" he answered as he went back to putting it together. I watched him for a few minutes and then I put away the dishes, silverware, pots, pans, etc… "What'da ya think?" he asked after he finished putting it together…

"It's cute…"

"We can sit here and have coffee…"

"Yea…" I said as I put the coffee pot and the Keurig on the counter…

"Why'd you want a Keurig and a coffee pot?"

"Sometimes I want a quick cup – but I love the smell of a fresh pot of coffee..."

"You do?"

"Yes – my mother used to make a pot of coffee every morning for my father and the house would smell so good..."

"That's when you know you're home..."

"Exactly..."

"So... you wanna inflate this mattress?"

"I thought you said we were going out?"

"We are... but I'm curious..." Wayne said as he came over to me and held me...

"Okay..." I sighed. Wayne took it out of the box, spread it out, and pushed the button to inflate it... "Hmm... it looks like a real bed..."

"It looks comfortable too..." When it got firm Wayne reached down to push on it...

"It feels comfortable..."

"I bet it is..."

"You ever sleep on one of these before?"

"I've slept on the ones that are lower to the floor..."

"Are they comfortable?"

"Not really..."

"Well... here goes..." Wayne said as he laid on it...

"Hmmm... it's comfortable..."

"You think you can sleep on it?"

"C'mere..." he said as he opened his arms...

"Okay..." I said as I knelt down onto the mattress and laid in his arms...

"That's better..." he said...

"This is comfortable..."

"Get on your back..."

"Okay..." I said as I got on my back...

"Spread your legs..."

"Okay..." I breathed as Wayne laid down on top of me and we started kissing...

"Yea... I think this'll work..."

"Me too..."

"It'll only be for a night or two – we'll have our real bed before the end of the week..." he breathed as he opened my zipper...

"Mmmm... okay..." I breathed as he pushed my pants and panties down off my waist and removed them...

"Spread your legs..." he said as he opened his pants, took his dick out, and eased it inside me... and I started to laugh... "Why are you laughing?"

"Because... it feels... like... wait..."

"Okay..."

"Get on your back... I'll show you..."

"Okay..." I got up, climbed on top of him, sat on his dick, started riding him... and he started laughing... "I... see... what... you... mean..."

"Oh shit..." I moaned...

"You like it Mommy?" he breathed as he grabbed my waist and held me down on his dick...

"Hell yea..." I breathed as I rode his dick...

"Yea... you like this... you're so fuckin' wet..."

"I'm about ready to cum..." I moaned...

"Cum for Daddy..."

"Oh... oh... oh... Fuck... I'm cumming... I'm cumming... Aaaaahhhh!"

"Yes Mommy... you haven't cum like that in a while..." Wayne breathed as he held me down on his dick...

"Oh my God... that was so fuckin' good..."

"I love this bed..."

"So do I..."

"Get on your back..."

"Okay..." I breathed as I got off his dick and got on my back...

"Spread your legs Mommy..."

"Yes Daddy..." I breathed as he eased himself inside me...

"Yes Mommy... damn your pussy feels good..." he breathed as he started fucking me hard...

"You like it Daddy?"

"Fuck yea..." he growled as he went deeper...

"Ooohhh..."

"How's it feel Mommy?"

"It feels good Daddy..." I moaned... "Why are you stopping?"

"Turn over..." he commanded... as he got up on his knees...

"Yes Daddy..." I breathed. Wayne spread my ass cheeks and I knew I was in for it... "Ooohhh..." I moaned as he eased his dick in my ass...

"Yes Mommy..." he moaned as he started fucking my ass... "Oh shit... Fuck..." he moaned...

"Daddy... I'm cumming again..."

"I'm cumming with you...

"Oh God... Oh God..."

"Mommy... Yes..."

"Fuck me! I'm cumming!"

"Uggh! Uggh! Uggh! Uggh!"

"Aaaaahhhh!"

"Uuugggghhhhh!"

"I love this bed!" I breathed as Wayne collapsed on top of me...

"I love you... in this bed..." Wayne breathed as he got up, turned me over on my back, and laid back down beside me...

"I love you too..."

"You still wanna go out?"

"Yea..."

"Okay... let's get up..."

"You first – we both can't get up at the same time..." I laughed...

"Okay..." he laughed as he got up...

"Help me up..." I laughed as I put up my hand...

"I gotcha..." he said as he pulled me up into his arms...

"I need to go... I'll be right back..." I said as I hurried to the bathroom... "Hmmm... I should take this pregnancy test while I'm in here..." I said as I got the test, opened it, sat down on the toilet, and peed on it... "Hurry up..." I said out loud...

"Everything alright?" Wayne asked...

"Yea... I'll be out in a minute..." I said as I looked at the stick... "Oh shit... I'm pregnant..."

Chapter 7

"What's taking you so long?" Wayne laughed as he came into the bathroom...

"I needed to freshen up a bit..." I answered. To be honest, I did need to freshen up – but I also needed to hide the pregnancy test from him...

"I might as well freshen up too...' he said as he reached for a washcloth right where I hid the pregnancy test...

"Umm... okay..."

"What's wrong with you?"

"Nothing... I'll go get dressed..."

"Mary... wait..."

"Yes Wayne?"

"Sit down... keep me company..."

"Okay..." I said as I sat on the toilet...

"You sure you're okay?"

"Yea... I'm just happy..."

"So am I..." he said as he bent down to kiss me... "Okay – I'm done – let's go..." he said as he grabbed my hand and pulled me off the toilet...

"Wayne... wait a minute..." I laughed...

"I want us to get there before it gets dark..." Wayne said as he got dressed in a hurry...

"Where are we going?" I asked as I got dressed...

"I'll tell you in the car – c'mon!"

"Okay, okay..." I laughed as we went out the door...

"Okay – where are we going?" I exclaimed...

"We're going to the Bayview Farm... in Kingston...

"You're taking me to a farm... on our anniversary?"

"Yes..."

"Well... that's a first..." I sighed as I settled into my seat. I was so excited I was pregnant I didn't give a damn where we were going or what we were doing. It took everything in me not to blurt it out in the car – thank God I had the view to occupy my thoughts until we got to the farm...

"We're here..." Wayne said as we pulled into the parking lot...

"Oh wow – it's beautiful!" I exclaimed...

"It is... isn't it?" he said as he pulled me into a kiss...

"I love you Mr. Robinson..."

"I love you too Mrs. Robinson..."

"Let's go inside and get a table..."

"Okay..." I breathed as he put his arm around me and we walked inside...

"Welcome to Bayview Farm – please have a seat wherever you like..." the owner said as he greeted us...

"This is absolutely perfect..." I sighed...

"Is this your first time here?"

"Yes..." Wayne answered...

"Oh wow – we love new customers – welcome to our family..."

"Thank you..." Wayne said as we both sat down...

"My wife will be right with you..." he said as he walked away...

"Mary... why are you crying?"

"I'm crying because I'm happy..."

"Welcome to Bayview Farm – I'll be taking your order – and your picture..." the wife said as she came over to greet us...

"You'll be taking our picture?" I asked...

"Yes... if that's alright – we take pictures of all our family..."

"What's your name?" Wayne asked...

"I'm Donna – and that's my husband Bill..."

"I'm Wayne – and this is my wife Mary..."

"Today's our anniversary..." I said...

"Oh my – Bill – we need champagne – it's their anniversary!" Donna exclaimed...

"I'll be right there Dear..." he said...

"So how long have you been married?"

"Two weeks..." Wayne answered...

"Did you say two weeks?" Bill asked as he brought the bottle of champagne to the table along with four glasses...

"Okay – Bill's gonna pour you each a glass of champagne – I'll take a picture of you both as you toast – then I'll take a picture with your phone – then I'll put my camera down and we'll have a toast with ya..." Donna laughed...

"Fine by me..." Wayne said as bill poured us champagne...

"Here's to us..." Wayne said as he raised his glass...

"To us..." I repeated as I raised my glass...

"Okay – hold that pose!" Donna said as she took the picture...

"Okay – where's your phone?"

"In my bag..." I answered...

"Okay – give me your phone – and give me that pose..." Donna said...

"Okay..." I said as I gave her the phone, gave her the pose, and she took the picture...

"Now – let's all toast..." Bill said as he poured glasses of champagne for the two of them and then they both sat with us...

"Come closer – I wanna get a selfie with all of us..." I said as they got closer and I took the picture...

"I'm gonna post that and check in on facebook..." I said...

"Oh that's great – thanks!" Bill said...

"So... what would you like for dinner?" Donna asked...

"We haven't seen a menu..." Wayne laughed...

"Oh my goodness – I forgot – well – I know that menu like the back of my hand – I'll put in an order for our Feature Appetizer-Stirling Water Buffalo Croquettes, Nepalese Potato Salad, and Burt's Baby Greens..."

"That sounds delicious..." I said...

"Trust me – you won't be disappointed..." she said as she went to place the order and get us menus...

"Thank you..." I said...

"For what?" Wayne asked...

"For loving me, wanting me, and marrying me..."

"Mary?"

"Yes Wayne?"

"Let's have a wedding..."

"You mean it?"

"Yes – I wanna have the wedding you've always wanted – we can have it here – what'da ya say?"

"Did you just ask me to marry you... again?" Wayne got up from his chair, came over to me, got down on one knee, and took my hand...

"Mary... will you marry me... again... here?"

"Yes..." I cried... "Yes – I'll marry you... again..."

"I'm gonna love you... want you... and marry you... again..." he said between kisses...

"Here's your appetizers – oh my goodness – what'd I miss?" Donna asked...

"I just asked my wife to marry me again – here – at the Bayview..." Wayne answered...

"Oh that's wonderful?"

"We got married at City Hall – this time next year I wanna give my wife the wedding she's always wanted..."

"Honey – I don't know where you found him – but he's a keeper!"

"God sent him to me..." I said...

"Aww... that's beautiful..." she said...

"This looks delicious..." Wayne said...

"It is – take a look at the menu and let me know what you'd like – I'll give you a few minutes..." she said as she went back to the kitchen...

"I see what I want..." I said...

"What?" Wayne asked...

"I'm gonna have their Feature Main Course-Quinn's Pork Loin Scallopine Lemon, Asparagus, Kelly's Wolfe Island Mushrooms Risotto, Crosswinds Lemon Thyme Cream..."

"Wow... that sounds delicious..."

"What are you getting?"

"I'm getting the Enright Filet Mignon, Hasselback Potatoes, Yorkshire Pudding, Allum, Demi Glace..."

"Ooohhh... that sounds good too..."

"Have you decided?" Donna asked...

"We have..." I answered...

"What'll it be?"

"I'll have your feature main course..."

"Excellent choice – you won't be disappointed – and for your Wayne?"

"I'll have your filet mignon..."

"Okay! Enjoy your appetizers - I'll be back!" Donna said as she went into the kitchen...

"This is really good..." Wayne said...

"It sure is..." I agreed...

"Chandler and Starr will love it here..."

"And so will the twins..."

"Oh – that's right!"

"I can't wait to get back to bed..."

"Tired? Already?" Wayne laughed...

"Not tired..." I answered as I smiled mischievously. We finished our appetizers just in time...

"Here's your dinner..." Donna said as she put our food on the table...

"Oh wow! Look at all this food!" I exclaimed...

"Enjoy!" Donna said as she walked away...

"I can't wait to get everything settled..." Wayne said...

"We don't have to rush..."

"Yes we do..."

"Why?"

"Because – once I start work I don't want to have to deal with it - and I don't want you to have to deal with it…"

"I'll be fine…"

"We'll talk about it more later – let's eat…"

"Okay…" It was getting harder and harder to keep from blurting out I was pregnant – thank God I had plenty of food to eat. I watched Wayne eat until his plate was clean… "Hungry huh?" I laughed…

"Yea… I guess I worked up an appetite…" he answered as he smiled at me mischievously…

"Can I get you anything else?" Donna asked…

"Oh no – I don't have room for anything else…" Wayne laughed…

"Me either…" I laughed…

"Okay – here's your check…" she said as she left the check on the table… "Welcome to the family…"

"Thank you…" we said in unison…

"You're welcome – have a good night…" she said as we went to pay the check and leave. When we got to the car I couldn't hold it in any longer…

"Wayne – I'm pregnant!" I yelled as I threw my arms around his neck…

"Pregnant? Oh wow…"

"I can't believe it!"

"Let's go home…" Wayne said as he kissed me…

"I love you…"

"I love you too…" Wayne said as he unlocked the door and got in. I ran around to the passenger side, opened the door, got in, and continued…

"I can't believe we're gonna have a baby – after all these years!"

"I'm shocked…" Wayne said…

"It's a miracle…"

"It certainly is…" Wayne agreed. I laid my head on Wayne's shoulder and dreamed about our child as Wayne drove. When we got home and I got out the car, I started up again…

"We're having a baby…"

"Yes we are – let's get inside…" Wayne said as he unlocked the door, opened it, went inside, and I followed…

"We're gonna have a baby!" I squealed as I closed the door, pushed him up against it, and kissed him…

"Mary… stop…"

"Wayne – it'll be great – we have three bedrooms – we can turn one of the bedrooms into a nursery – we'll still have our office – oh my God – I'm so happy…"

"Mary… it's not mine…"

"What?"

"It's not mine…" he whispered with tears in his eyes…

"Wayne… how could you say that… I haven't been with anyone else…" I said as I started to cry…

"Mary…" Wayne cried as he took my hands and kissed them… "Nothing would make me happier… but it isn't mine…"

"Wayne… please… I love you… I haven't been with anyone else… I swear…"

"Mary… I love you… I know how much you love me… I'm not accusing you of cheating…"

"Why are you saying this to me then?"

"Sit down…" Wayne said as he sat at the table. I sat down at the table and looked at him with tear-soaked eyes… "After I found out Starr wasn't my daughter… I went to see a doctor…"

"You did – why?"

"We were together for 18 years… you never got pregnant after Starr…"

"I know…"

"I needed to know why… for myself…"

"I always thought there was something wrong with me…"

"It's not you… it's me…"

"You can't have children?"

"The doctor did a complete exam. After he checked my testicles, my prostate, and my semen the doctor sent me for a testicular ultrasound…"

"A testicular ultrasound?"

"They did a sonogram of my scrotum…"

"Ohh… okay – so you lay on your back and spread your legs?"

"Yes – they put a towel underneath my scrotum to keep it elevated, put the gel on, and did the same thing to me that they do to pregnant women..."

"Oooohhh... okay..."

"I have Congenital Bilateral Absence of the Vas Deferens..."

"What does that even mean?"

My testicles are normal... but my Vas Deferens... the tubes that carry sperm... didn't develop properly..."

"I've swallowed... you ejaculate semen..."

"Yes... I do ejaculate semen... but my tubes didn't develop properly... so my sperm doesn't get transported to become part of my semen..."

"So your sperm just sits there?"

"Yes..."Wayne whispered as he cried...

"Wayne... I'm sorry..." I cried...

"It's not your fault..."

"I didn't mean to hurt you... again..."

"C'mere..." Wayne said as he got up, pulled me into a hug, and we held each other...

"I'm pregnant... by Jermoll..." I cried...

"We're gonna get through this Mary... I promise..."

"You're not leaving me?"

"I'll never leave you again..."

"Oh Wayne... I don't deserve you..."

"Ssshhhh... I love you..."

"I love you too..."

"Mary... I need to tell you something..." he said as he sat down...

"Yes Wayne?"

"I don't want to hurt you..."

"Okay..."

"Please... don't hate me..."

"Never..."

"I don't want to do this..."

"You don't want the baby?"

"No..."

"Oh my God..." I said as I started to cry...

"I'm not sure I can go through this again..."

"You love Starr... and she's not your daughter..."

"Starr is my daughter... and yes... I love her..."

"You don't think you can love this baby?"

"Mary... of course I can love this baby... I'm just not sure I can do this... again..."

"It's not fair... what about what I want?"

"I thought you wanted me..."

"I do want you... but I also want this baby..."

"Mary... I love you... but I just can't... not again..." he said as he started to cry..."

"I understand... you don't want it... because it's not yours... I get it..."

"Mary... please... you don't know what I went through when I found out Starr wasn't my daughter..."

"I'm sorry…"

"I know… I forgive you… but you broke my heart…"

"I'm sorry!" I cried…

"Mary…" Wayne said as he took my hands… "I love you… that's in the past… but this… this is bringing all the hurt back to the surface… I just can't do it… I'm sorry…"

"So you want me to get an abortion?"

"Yes… I'm sorry…" he whispered as he cried…

"Okay… I'll get an abortion…" I said as I got up…

"Where are you going?"

"I'M GOINT TO GET THE LAPTOP - AND FIND AN ABORTION CLINIC!"

Chapter 8

"Mary,

I went to check us out of the hotel. You were sleeping so peacefully I didn't want to disturb you. I'll be back later.

Love,

Wayne"

After he left the note on the table he slipped out the door, closed it quietly, and went to get in the car. He drove to the hotel in silence, parked the car, went into the hotel, and headed for the lounge...

"I might as well get myself some coffee..." he thought to himself as he made the coffee and went upstairs to the room. When he got in the room and closed the door, he couldn't hold it in anymore – he fell to the floor on his knees and sobbed...

"God... please... help me..."

"Yes Wayne..."

"I fucked up..."

"No you didn't..."

"I hurt her so bad... I didn't mean to..."

"I know..."

"It's not fair! Why couldn't that be my child?' Why me? Haven't I suffered enough?"

"It is your child... and... as far as your suffering... that's your choice..."

"I don't understand..."

"You've always wanted children... I've given you another chance... and... instead of realizing how blessed you are... you're suffering..."

"I want to be happy... I love children... but I just can't..."

"You just can't be happy with your wife being pregnant... or... is it that you just can't forgive Bazil?"

"Lord... this isn't about Bazil..."

"Did you forget who you're talking to?" You told your wife you couldn't go through this again... you also told your wife that this was bringing up past hurt... so if it's not about Bazil... who's it about?"

"I never thought of it that way..."

"I know..."

"I love her so much... I just want that baby to be mine..."

"Then why did you tell her to have an abortion?"

"I don't know... I can't deal with it... it broke my heart with Starr..."

"You love Starr... don't you?"

"Yes..."

"You told your wife you forgive her... right?"

"Yes..."

"You're not treating your wife like you forgive her..."

"I know... I'm sorry... I don't know what to do..."

"You know exactly what to do... it's just a matter of what you choose..."

"Lord... I'm not sure I can do this..."

"Wayne... do you trust me?"

"Yes Lord... I trust you..."

"Show me..." Wayne jumped up off the floor, grabbed the suitcases, threw everything in them without bothering to fold the clothes, and hurried out the room.

"Good morning Mr. Robinson – I see you have suitcases – are you finally checking out?" the clerk asked...

"Yes I am..."

"Congratulations... we'll miss you..."

"Thank you..."

"Think you'll be back anytime soon?" she asked as she completed his check out and gave him the paperwork...

"Only God knows…" he answered as he grabbed the paperwork and hurried out the hotel…

"Wayne?" I called out as I rolled over… "Hmmm… I guess he's not here…" I said as I got up off the bed and went to the bathroom. When I came out the bathroom I saw the note on the table, picked it up, and read it…

"Mary,

I went to check us out of the hotel. You were sleeping so peacefully I didn't want to disturb you. I'll be back later.

Love,

Wayne"

"I love you too…" I whispered… "Might as well get ready to go…" I said as I got ready to take a shower. I didn't wait long enough for the water to get hot – once it was luke warm, I just got in, took a quick shower, and got out. Thank God I didn't have to worry about ironing because that's another thing we forgot to buy – an iron. I got dressed, went outside, ordered an uber, waited until I saw the uber pull up, and then I got in…

"Good morning…" the driver said as I got in…

"Good morning…" I replied…

"You're going to Planned Parenthood?"

"Yes I am…"

"Are you pregnant?"

"Are we fucking?"

"Excuse me Maam?"

"Are we fucking?" I repeated...

"Why would you ask me that?"

"Why would you ask me if I'm pregnant?"

"I was just trying to make conversation..." We rode in silence the rest of the way – musta been something I said – ha ha! When we got to Planned Parenthood he didn't say anything – he just parked and waited for me to get out...

"Have a nice day!" I said as I got out and went inside...

"Welcome to Planned Parenthood – how may I help you?" the young lady asked. I looked around without answering... "Here ya go – just fill these out – my name's Gina – when you're donc, bring them back to me – I'll make up a chart and someone will be out to see you..."

"Thank you Gina..." I said as I took the clipboard, looked at the forms, and started crying...

"You okay?" a young girl whispered as she touched my shoulder...

"No..." I whispered as I shook my head...

"Here..." she said as she offered me a pack of tissues...

"Thanks..."

"You'll be alright..." she said as they called her name and she went down the hall. I filled out all the questions, went back to the counter, and gave Gina the clipboard...

"Someone will see you soon..." Gina said as she touched my hand to comfort me. I sat down and continued to cry silently as I took out my phone, went on facebook, and waited to be called...

"Mary Robinson?"

"Yes – I'm Mary Robinson..." I answered as I stood up...

"Come with me please..." she said as I followed her down the hall and into an examination room... "Come here..." she said as she pulled me into a hug and I cried on her shoulder for a few minutes... "Have a seat..." I wiped my eyes and sat down... "My name's Carol..."

"Hi Carol..." I sniffed...

"I've looked over your chart..."

"Okay..."

"You stated that you're here for an abortion..."

"Yes... that's correct..." I answered as I started crying again...

"Are you sure about this?"

"Yes..."

"You don't seem like you're sure..."

"My husband doesn't want the baby..." I cried...

"Oh my God... I'm so sorry... he doesn't want children?"

"He loves children..."

"Then why doesn't he want his child?"

"I can't..."

"Mary..." she said as she took my hand... "Whatever you tell me stays between us – it doesn't go in your file and we don't tell the doctor..."

"Okay..."

"You wanna talk about it?"

"Maybe..."

"Maybe? Is that a yes?"

"Yea..."

"Good... what's wrong?"

"He doesn't want the baby... because... it's not his!" I cried...

"Mary..." she said as she put my head on her shoulder... "You're not the first woman to make a mistake..."

"I didn't make a mistake..."

"I don't understand..."

"We've been married two weeks – we just got back together – I was with someone else – I didn't know I was pregnant..."

"Did you explain this to your husband?"

"I didn't have to..."

"Why not?"

"My husband knows it's not his baby because he can't have children..."

"Ohhhh... I see..."

"I don't want to have an abortion... but he told me last night he doesn't want the baby..." I said as I started crying again...

"Mary..."

"Yes?"

"I'm going to make a suggestion..."

"Okay..."

"Wait a minute..."

"Okay..."

"I mean – you should wait a minute..."

"Okay..."

"You've only been married two weeks – give your husband some time to process what you've told him – it's a lot to process for both of you..."

"Okay..."

"I'm going to take a urine sample, some blood, I'm gonna do a pelvic exam, and an ultrasound – we'll take it from there – you don't have to do anything today – okay?"

"Okay..."

"There's a cup in the bathroom – give me some urine, write your name on the cup, and come back in here..."

"Okay..." I sniffed as I got up and went to the bathroom. Thank God the bathroom was clean – a clean bathroom reduces my anxiety – especially when it comes to public bathrooms. After I peed in the cup, I wrote my name on it and went back to the room....

"Thanks..." Carol said as she took the urine from me... "Okay – I'm gonna take some blood now – have you eaten anything?"

"No..."

"Would you like some coffee?"

"Yes..."

"How do you like it?"

"Light and sweet..."

"Okay – I'll get some blood – and then I'll get you some coffee..."

"Okay..." I said as I watched her prepare the tubes and the needle...

"You okay?"

"Yes... I'm okay..."

"I always ask – some people don't like needles..." she said as she took my blood... "I'll be right back with your coffee..." she said as she took the blood, took the urine, and left the room...

"Gina – do we have any coffee left?"

"Yes Carol..."

"Good – I need a cup – light and sweet – asap!"

"Is it for Mary?"

"Yes..."

"She okay?" Gina asked as she made a cup of coffee and gave it to Carol..."

"She's as well as can be expected..." Carol answered as she went back down the hall...

"Here ya go..." Carol said as she gave me the coffee..."

"Thank you..." I breathed as I started gulping it down...

"Careful – it's hot!"

"I don't care..." I breathed as I finished it...

"I guess you needed that..."

"I did..."

"Okay – I'm going to do a pelvic exam – I need you to get undressed from the waist down – I'll leave if you want..."

"No – that's okay..." I said as I undressed and got back up on the table...

"Okay – scoot down a bit so we can see what's going on..." she said. I scooted down and she proceeded with a quick pelvic exam – by the time I felt her fingers inside me she was finished...

"Wow – that was quick..."

"Everything feels okay – now let's see how everything looks..." she said as she squirted the gel on my stomach, turned on the machine, and started doing the sonogram... "Hmmm..."

"Is everything okay?"

"It's hard to tell what's going on – I need to do a transvaginal ultrasound..."

"What's a transvaginal ultrasound?"

"I'm going to put this long tube in your vagina – it will help me see your uterus, fallopian tubes, ovaries, cervix, and your vagina..."

"Will it hurt?"

"No – it doesn't use radiation – you might feel a little discomfort as I'm putting the transducer in, but that's it…"

"Okay…"

"Are you ready?"

"Yes…"

"Take a deep breath… then relax…" she said as she put the transducer in my vagina… "Look… see that tiny little peanut right there?"

"Yes… I see it…"

"That's your baby…"

"I know…" I whispered as I started crying again…

"Do you want a picture?"

"Yes…" I sniffed…

"Okay… I'll print one out for you…" she said as she printed the picture for me…

"Can I get up now?"

"Yes Mary – I'm finished…" she answered as I started getting dressed…

"How far along am I Carol?"

"I'd say you're about 2 weeks…"

"Okay…" I sighed…

"Okay – we've done the urine, the blood, the pelvic exam, the ultrasound. And the transvaginal ultrasound – now we need to talk about the abortion…"

"Okay…" I said as my eyes started tearing up…

"There are two categories of abortion…"

"Okay..." I said as tears ran down my cheeks...

"Medical is where we use medication that causes the uterus to expel the pregnancy. Surgical is where the clinician removes the pregnancy..." I continued crying as she continued... "The Medical Abortion uses a pill – it's similar to a miscarriage – you cramp, there's heavy bleeding, it can take longer, and require more appointments..."

"Oh my God... I can't..." I whispered...

"The Surgical Abortion feels more invasive, has more pain management, and is available quicker with fewer appointments. If you decide you want to go through with an abortion, you'll receive information on both procedures that explains the side effects and consequences. Before you get the abortion, both procedures require an education session and counseling..."

"I don't need education or counseling..." I said...

"Mary..." it's mandatory..."

"I'm not doing it..."

"We'll give you all the information... in case you change your mind..."

"Carol – you've been very compassionate – I appreciate your kindness – but I've heard enough – I'm not having an abortion..."

"What about your husband?"

"I'm gonna pray God will change his mind..." I sighed as I got up to leave...

"Mary – wait…" Carol said as she stopped me by taking my hand…

"Yes Carol?"

"Please… just take the information… show it to your husband… whatever you decide… you shouldn't make this decision alone…"

"You know what – you're right – I'll take the information – and I'll show it to my husband – and then I'll tell him I'm not having an abortion…" I said as I took the information and walked out the room…

"Good for you Mary… good for you…" Carol said to herself…

"Lord… please… I don't want to do this…" I cried…

"I know you don't…"

"I love him so much…"

"He loves you too…"

"I didn't mean to hurt him again…"

"He knows that… and so do I…"

"I just want my husband… and I want my baby… why can't I have both?"

"You said you don't want to hurt him… right?"

"Yes…"

"You're his wife… he's your husband… if you don't want to hurt him… stop telling him it's your baby… remind him how much he loves children… remind him what a wonderful father he is… let him know what a wonderful father he'll be…"

"I want to… but I'm scared… what if he won't listen?"

"Do you trust me?"

"Yes Lord… I trust you…"

"Show me…"

Chapter 9

"Oh my God! Everybody out! Now!" Gina screamed...

"Gina! What's happening?" Carol asked as she came running down the hall...

"There's a bomb! Everybody out!" Gina screamed again as everybody scrambled to get out...

"Boom!"

"Oh my God! Dr. Berkley!" Carol screamed as she tried to run back down the hall...

"Carol! Get out!" Gina screamed as she dragged her out the entrance...

"Boom!" They made it out just in time...

"Maam – we need to get you ladies away from the building..." the fire chief said as two firemen pulled them away. They watched from across the street as the firetrucks tried their best to put the fire out but it had already gotten out of control. The Bomb Squad, Swat, and the FBI showed up along with the local news...

"This is Ken Shaw, CTV News, Toronto. We interrupt our regularly scheduled programming to bring you this news. Moments ago, there was an explosion at Planned Parenthood. Tracy Tong is on the scene – go ahead Tracy…"

"Excuse me… Maam… do you work here at Planned Parenthood?"

"Yes…" Gina sniffed…

"What's your name Maam?"

"Gina…"

"Can you tell us what happened?" the reporter asked as she put a microphone in Gina's face…

"I… got… a… call…" Gina stuttered… "He said there was a bomb… he said we had 5 minutes to get out… Oh my God!" Gina cried…

"Did he say anything else Maam?"

"He said to let everyone know… he was part of the Army of God…" she cried…

"I'm Tracy Tong, CTV News, Toronto – we're here at Planned Parenthood where an employee has just confirmed that this was an attack by the domestic terrorist group known as the Army of God. The Army of God is an underground network of domestic terrorists that believe the use of violence is appropriate and acceptable as a means to end abortion – back to you Ken…"

"This is Ken Shaw, CTV News, Toronto. CTV News will continue to keep you posted. We now return to our regularly scheduled programming."

"Mary! Oh my God… my wife…"

"Your wife?" she was here?"

"Yes… Oh God… please don't let me loose her!" Wayne cried…

"Wait here…" Sergeant Gallagher said as he went to talk to the FBI… and Wayne saw the body bags…

"Maaarrryyyy! Nooooo!" Wayne cried as he ran towards them…

"Mr. Robinson – I know you're upset – but I need you to stay back!" Sergeant Gallagher snapped as he grabbed Wayne by the collar and held him in a bear hug…

"Please… I can't lose her… let me go… I need to see if she's in there…"

"Mr. Robinson – come with me…" Sergeant Gallagher said as he took Wayne over to his car…

"Am I being arrested?"

"No…"

"Why am I sitting in your car?"

"Because… you need to call Chandler…"

"I can't…"

"I can call him for you… if you want…"

"Oh God… she's pregnant…"

"Your wife?"

"Yes…"

"I'll call Chandler…" Sergeant Gallagher said as he dialed Chandler's number…

"This is Chandler…"

"Chandler… this is Chris…"

"Chris?"

"Chris Gallagher…"

"Oh – hey Chris…"

"Chandler… I'm sorry to call you under these circumstances…"

"What's wrong?" Chandler asked…

"Chandler… what's wrong?" Starr asked…

"Starr – wait a minute – go 'head Chris…"

"There was a terrorist attack at Planned Parenthood…"

"An attack?" What happened?"

"The clinic was bombed…"

"Oh wow…"

"Mrs. Robinson was at the clinic…"

"Chris… are you calling me to tell me my wife's mother is dead?"

"Oh my God! Mooommmmyyyy!" Starr screamed as she broke down crying…

"Chandler – open the door!" Charles yelled. Chandler ran to the door, unlocked it, then ran back over to Starr and tried to console her…

"Chandler? Chandler? Are you there?"

"Yes – I'm here…" he answered as he started crying…

"We don't know for sure – they've taken a few bodies out in bags – we don't know yet…"

"Is Wayne there?"

"He's here…"

"Le'me talk to him…"

"Wayne – its Chandler…" Sergeant Gallagher said as he handed him the phone…

"Chandler…" Wayne cried…

"Wayne... what happened?"

"I came here to get Mary... there was an explosion... I can't find her... Oh God... I can't lose her..."

"Chandler?" Sergeant Gallagher took the phone away from Wayne...

"Yes... I'm here..."

"We won't know anything until we identify the bodies..."

"When?"

"We'll need Wayne to come down to the morgue..."

"Oh my God... le'me speak to him..."

"He's a mess Chandler – I'm gonna take him home..."

"He didn't drive?"

"He's in no condition to drive – I'll make sure he gets home – with his car – I'll keep you posted – I gotta go..." Sergeant Gallagher said as he hung up...

"Chandler... is my mother dead?" Starr asked...

"They don't know..." Chandler answered as he started crying...

"Moommmyyy!" Starr screamed as she fell into Chandler's arms...

"Charles? Are you here?" Theresa asked as she came inside...

"Theresa!" Starr cried...

"Starr – Oh my God... what happened?" Theresa asked as she ran over to Starr and hugged her...

"It's my mother..."

"What happened?" Theresa mouthed to Chandler...

"I don't know..." Chandler mouthed back.

Chapter 10

"Waaaahhhh!"

"Oh my God – Jay – Mommy's coming!" Beautiee exclaimed as she jumped up and ran into his room...

"Waaaahhhh!"

"What's wrong?" Bazil asked as he came running into the room...

"I don't know..." Beautiee answered as she picked Jay up and tried to console him...

"Waaaahhhh!"

"Maybe he's hungry..." Bazil suggested...

"That's not it – he doesn't scream like this when he's hungry..."

"Shoot – that's my phone – I'll be right back..."

"Jay... calm down... Mommy's here..." Beautiee said as she started to rock him...

"Waaaahhhh!"

"Beautiee – we need to go – now!"

"Bazil – you're scaring me – what's wrong?"

"It's Chandler..." he snapped as he flew downstairs. Beautiee grabbed Jay's diaper bag and hurried downstairs behind Bazil...

"Waaaahhhh!"

"Something's wrong..." Beautiee said as she put Jay in the car seat and then got in the car...

"I know..." Bazil said...

"I think Jay can feel it..."

"Waaaahhhh!"

"Really?"

"Yes – that's why he won't stop crying..."

"Hmmmm... is that why you're crying Jay?" Bazil asked...

"Uh huh..." Jay sniffed...

"We're almost there Jay... calm down... stop crying... okay?"

"Okay... Daddy..." Jay said as he calmed down...

"Chandler – we're downstairs – I'm parking now..." Bazil said...

"Good – hurry up – Starr needs you..."

"We're on our way..." Bazil said as he hung up his cell and they got out the car...

"What'd he say?" Beautiee asked as they got in the elevator...

"He said Starr needs us..."

"Dad? Is that you?" Chandler asked as he went to open the door...

"Yes Chandler..."

"Thank God..." Chandler said as he opened the door and let them in...

"Where is she?"

"She's..."

"Daddy!" Starr cried as she ran to hug Bazil...

"Starr..." Bazil whispered as he started crying... "What's wrong?"

"Waaaahhhh!"

"Mommy might be dead!" she cried...

"Waaaahhhh!"

"Starr... Come here..." Beautiee said as she pulled Starr into a hug..."

"Why is Jay crying?" Starr asked as she took him from Beautiee and held him...

"I think he knows you're upset..." Beautiee answered...

"Chandler – le'me talk to you a minute..." Bazil said as he took Chandler into the living room and they both sat down on the couch... "What's going on?"

"Sigh... I got a call from Sergeant Gallagher..." Chandler whispered...

"Okay..."

"There was a terrorist attack on Planned parenthood in Ontario..."

"Okay..."

"The clinic was bombed..."

"Oh God... no..."

"Wayne can't find Mary..."

"She was there?"

"Yea..."

"Where's Wayne now?"

"Sergeant Gallagher said he's in no condition to drive – he's gonna make sure Wayne gets home…"

"Have they identified anyone yet?"

"Sergeant Gallagher said they won't know anything until they identify the bodies…"

"Did you tell Starr this?"

"No… I can't…"

"Okay – I need to make a call – I'll be right back…" Bazil said as he got up and went out into the hallway…

"Where's my father going?" Starr asked…

"He needs to make a call – he'll be right back…" Chandler answered…

"Hey Bazil…"

"There was a terrorist attack on Planned parenthood…"

"Where?"

"Ontario…"

"Oh shit…"

"He can't find Mary…"

"Oh shit!"

"My daughter's distraught…"

"I'll see what I can find out – I'll call you as soon as I know anything…"

"Thank you Conrad…"

"Anybody hungry? I can cook something…" Theresa said…

"Theresa – that's sweet of you – but you don't have to do that…" Beautiee said…

"We're all pregnant – we all need to eat – especially you Starr…" Theresa said…

"I'll cook…" Bazil said…

"Dad – you don't have to do that…" Chandler said…

"Okay - that's it – somebody's gotta cook – and we all need to eat!" Beautiee said…

"I have a taste for pizza…" Starr said…

"Okay – pizza it is!" Beautiee said as she took out her phone… "Hello – I'd like a delivery please… uh huh… yes it is… okay – I'd like a large chicken broccoli, a Hawaiian, a philly steak and onions, a garlic bread, and a house special… yes… all large… hold on a minute – Bazil – give me your wallet.."

"Here…" Bazil said as he handed his wallet to her and she took out one of the credit cards…

"Okay – you ready for the number? Okay – 4008-1234-7890… 12/22… 878… okay – thank you…" Beautiee said as she hung up…

"You sure we eatin' all that pizza?" Charles asked…

"I'm sure…" Beautiee answered…

"Chandler – come next door with me a minute…"

"I need to be here with my wife…"

"Go 'head Chandler – we got her…" Beautiee said…

"Okay – I'll be right back…" Chandler said as he followed Charles next door…

"You want some Henney?" Charles asked…

"Hell yea…"

"Okay…" Charles said as he opened the bottle of Hennesey, poured two glasses, and handed one to Chandler. Chandler gulped down the Hennesey and slammed the glass back down on the table…

"Thanks – I needed that…" he breathed…

"I guess you did – le'me pour you another…" Charles said as he started to pour Chandler another drink but Chandler stopped him…

"Naa – I'm good…"

"Okay - well – at least let me catch up to you…" he said as he finished his drink and set the glass down on the table…

"I don't know what I'm gonna do if she's dead…" Chandler sighed…

"You can talk to me anytime – I'm here…" Charles said as he put his hand on Chandler's shoulder…

"Thanks – I appreciate that – thank God Starr has Beautiee…"

"She has Theresa too…"

"I know she does – but Beautiee's like a mother to her – and she's gonna need that…"

"Maybe not…"

"I hope you're right – she's so close to her mother I told her that her mother could move in with us..."

"What! Oh hell no! Are you crazy man?"

"Honestly?"

"Yea..."

"Hell yea I'm crazy!" Chandler laughed...

"Oh shit! So what happened? Why didn't she move in?"

"My wife told me, No Chandler – I've waited a long time for you – I prayed for you – and now we're getting married – I want you all to myself – I want to enjoy being your wife – I want to enjoy my husband – love my husband – and I don't want my mother anywhere near that!"

"Really?"

"Oh yea – she also said she wanted to be able to walk around how she wants to walk around..."

"I know that's right! She on her grown-woman shit!" Charles laughed... "But seriously – you were gonna let that go down?"

"If she wanted it..."

"You really love her – don't you?"

"Hell yea..."

"Everything's gonna be alright Chandler..."

"If you say so..."

"It is... come in – the door's open..." Charles said as he got up to go see who was at the door...

"Honey – the food's here – you want me to bring you a plate?" Theresa asked...

"No baby – I'll come get it – c'mon Chan – let's go..." Charles answered as he held the door open for Chandler and they went back next door...

"Chandler..." Starr exclaimed when she saw him...

"You okay?" Chandler asked as he pulled her into a hug...

"I'm better now... but I'll really be okay when Dad finds Mommy..." she answered as she laid her head on his chest and he held her...

"Where's Jay?" Chandler asked...

"He's in the crib..."

"Is he sleep?"

"No..."

"What's he doing?"

"He's playing with one of their toys..."

"Aww... that's cute..." Beautiee said as she opened all the boxes of pizza... "Okay – everybody eat..."

"Can we all hold hands first?" Starr asked. Nobody answered her – everyone just took somebody's hand until the circle was complete around the island... "God... thank you for this pizza..." she said and then she bust out laughing along with everyone else... "I'm hungry... and it smells so good..."

"It sure does..." Beautiee sighed...

"Thank you for my husband – I'm handling this better than I thought I would just because I'm near him..." Chandler wrapped his arm around her as she continued... "Thank you for our new friends, Charles and Theresa – they're really sweet..."

"Aww... ⁻ we love you too..." Theresa said...

"Thank you for my lil' brother – even when he's upset, he calms me down..."

"Yeeaaa!" Jay squealed from the crib and everyone laughed...

"Thank you for my parents – and thank you for giving my father Beautiee..."

"Starr..." Beautiee whispered as she teared up...

"And God... please help Dad find Mommy... Amen..."

"Amen!" they all said in unison as Bazil's phone rang...

"I'll be right back – I need to take this..." Bazil said as he stepped out into the hallway...

"Hello Conrad..."

"Hello Bazil..."

"Do you have something for me?"

"Maybe..."

"Tell me..."

"Two bodies were taken out in body bags..."

"Okay..."

"One was identified as Dr. Berkley..."

"Okay…"

"So the other body may not be Mary's…"

"You sound like you're sure…"

"There were a lot of people in the clinic – and only one person died besides the doctor – the rest of the patients were taken to the hospital for injuries…"

"So where the hell is Mary?" Bazil asked as Beautiee came out into the hall and closed the door behind her…

"Bazil?"

"Yes Beautiee?" he answered as he hung up on Conrad and put the phone in his pocket…

"C'mere…" she said as she pulled Bazil into a hug…

"I love you so much…" he breathed and then he kissed her…

"I love you too – come back inside before Starr gets suspicious…" she said as she took him by the hand and pulled him inside…

"There you are…" Starr said as she handed Bazil a plate with a slice of everything all piled up…

"Starr…" Bazil laughed… "I can't eat all this…"

"Beautiee will help you – right Beautiee?"

"Yes Starr – I'll help him…" Beautiee laughed as she picked up one of the slices and bit into it… "Oh my God… this is soooo good… thank you Starr…" she said as she continued eating…

"For what?"

"You're the one that wanted pizza..." Beautiee laughed...

"Oh yea... I did..." she said as she went back over to Theresa and started a conversation while they ate...

"You're a lucky man Chandler..." Charles said...

"Thank ya, thank ya..." Chandler acknowledged as they ate...

"She's gonna be okay Chandler..."

"You know what – you keep saying that – like you know something..."

"I just have a feeling..." Charles sighed.

Chapter 11

"I'll see you to the door..." Sergeant Gallagher said as he got out the car with Wayne...

"I'll be okay..." Wayne sighed...

"That wasn't a suggestion..." Sergeant Gallagher said...

"Yes Sir..." Wayne said as he went up the steps, put the key in the lock, opened the door... and screamed... "MAAARRRYYY!"

"Oh Wayne – I'm so happy you're home – I'm..." I couldn't say anything else because Wayne grabbed me, pulled me into a hug, and kissed me so hard I could barely breathe... and then he started crying...

"Johnson – get in here – now!" Sergeant Gallagher yelled and then he turned back towards the door and went inside... "Lady – you're a sight for sore eyes..." he said as he pulled me away from Wayne and pulled me into a hug...

"Sarge – is everything okay?" Officer Johnson breathed as he ran inside...

"This is Mary Robinson..." Sergeant Gallagher said as he introduced me...

"Oh my God – I'm so glad you're okay!" Officer Johnson said as he pulled me into a hug...

"Yes... I'm okay – now can somebody tell me what's going on?"

"I'm sorry – we need you to come down to the police station so you can give us a statement – I'm gonna go cancel the missing person's report – c'mon Johnson – let's give 'em a minute..." Sergeant Gallagher said as they went out to the car...

"Wayne – why are you crying? What's wrong?"

"Thank you God, Thank you..." Wayne cried as he pulled me into a hug and held me...

"Wayne..."

"Yes Mary?" Wayne answered and then he started kissing me all over my face, my eyes, my lips, my neck...

"Wayne..."

"Yes Mary..." he breathed as he tried to lay me down...

"Wayne!"

"Yes?"

"What's going on?"

"I'm sorry... I love you so much... I thought I lost you..." he cried and then he started kissing me again...

"Wayne... stop..."

"Okay... but we need to call Chandler... and Starr..."

"Why? Is something wrong?"

"I couldn't find you... I thought I lost you..."

"Wayne – you filed a missing person report on me – and you called Chandler?"

"Actually – Sergeant Gallagher called Chandler..."

"Wayne – I'm confused..."

"Let's call Chandler..." Wayne said and then he dialed Chandler before I could ask him anything else...

"Oh shit – Starr – Wayne's calling my phone – hang on..." Chandler said as he answered...

"Wayne?"

"Chandler – I found her!" he cried...

"Is she okay?"

"She's fine..."

"Hold on – I'ma put you on speaker..." Chandler said... "Aiight Wayne – go 'head..."

"I found her..." Wayne said again as he cried...

"Oh thank God!" Theresa said...

"I told you man!" Charles exclaimed...

"Dad! You found Mommy?" Starr asked...

"Yes Starr – your mother's right here..."

"Mommy!" Starr exclaimed as she bust out crying...

"Thank you Lord!" Beautiee exclaimed...

"Thank you Lord..." Bazil acknowledged...

"Hey everybody..." I said...

"Hey!" They all said in unison…

"Sound like you're having a hell of a party…" I laughed…

"Jay – guess what? Mommy's okay!" Starr squealed…

"Yeaaaa!" Jay squealed…

"Is that Jay?" I asked…

"That's Jay…" Beautiee answered…

"Well damn – it's nice to know I mean so much to y'all…" I said…

"Of course you do Mommy!" Starr said…

"Listen – Sergeant Gallaher's waiting for us – we gotta go – but before we go – Mary has something to tell you…" Wayne said…

"I do?"

"Yes you do – unless you want me to tell 'em…"

"I don't know what I'm supposed to say!" I laughed…

"Look-a-here – somebody gonna tell us – okay?" Chandler laughed…

"We're having a baby…" Wayne said…

"Oh my God! Mommy! You're pregnant?" Starr screamed…

"Yes Starr… I'm pregnant!" I screamed back…

"Oh my God! We're all pregnant!" Theresa screamed…

"All?" I asked…

"Yes Mary…" Beautiee answered…

"Good thing we're having a huge baby shower for all the mothers…" Starr laughed…

"Wait a minute – all the mothers?" I asked…

"Yes Mommy – Me, Theresa, Keisha, Beautiee, and you!"

"Wait a minute – Beautiee – you're pregnant too?"

"Yes Mary – I'm pregnant too…"

"Well damn – we're all gonna be in the maternity ward at the same time!" I laughed…

"I guess we'll meet you at the hospital then…" Beautiee said…

"Jay – you're gonna have another brother – or another sister!" Starr squealed…

"Yeaaa!" Jay squealed…

"I must be dreaming…" I said…

"Why Mommy?"

"Everybody's happy for me – even the baby's happy for me – thank you God!"

"Okay – we gotta go – we'll be in touch…" Wayne said as he hung up…

"Thank you God!" Starr exclaimed…

"Yes – thank you God!" Chandler exclaimed as he pulled Starr into a hug…

"Thank God!" they all said as they took turns hugging each other…

"I love you Daddy…" Starr said as she hugged Bazil…

"I love you too…" he said…

"I love you Beautiee..." she said as she hugged Beautiee...

"I love you too Starr..." Beautiee said. "Jay – time to go home..." she yawned as she took Jay from Starr and held him...

"Aww look... he's so cute!" Starr said as Jay yawned...

"I feel you Jay – I'm tired too..." Theresa yawned...

"C'mon Babe – I'll put you to bed – good night y'all..." Charles yawned...

"Good night..." Starr and Chandler said in unison as they left...

"Good night Chandler..." Beautiee said as she hugged Chandler...

"Good night Beautiee... thank you..."

"You don't have to thank me Chandler..."

"Good night Chandler..." Bazil said as he hugged him...

"Good night Dad... thank you..."

"You're welcome... shoot – that's my phone – I need to take this..." Bazil said as he went out into the hall..."

"Why does Daddy keep doing that?" Starr asked...

"He's always on call – or something..." Beautiee answered...

"You don't mind?" Starr asked...

"I don't mind..." Beautiee answered... "I'm gonna go... we'll see you soon..." Beautiee said as she went out into the hall...

"Yes I know... thank you Conrad..." Beautiee heard Bazil say before he hung up...

"Conrad?" Beautiee asked...

"Yes..."

"Isn't that the attorney that represented Mary?"

"Yes..."

"C'mon – let's hurry up and get to the car – your son's heavy when he's sleeping..."

"Oh – so he's my son 'cause he's heavy?" Bazil laughed as they got in the elevator. Beautiee didn't answer him. The elevator went down to the main floor, the door opened, they got off, went through the lobby and out to the car... "Let me get the door for you..." Bazil said as he opened the door, took Jay out her arms, and put him in the car seat... "C'mere..." he said as he pulled Beautiee into a hug and held her... "What's wrong?"

"Nothing..." Beautiee sighed...

"Beautiee..." he breathed as he kissed her... "Tell me..."

"That's not Wayne's baby..."

"Oh wow... I never thought about that..."

"It's Jermoll's baby..."

"Beautiee..." he breathed as he kissed her again... "I gotchu..."

"I know..." she said as she looked up into his eyes and smiled...

"Are you okay?"

"Yea… I'm okay… he's dead… he can't hurt me anymore…" she said…

"Beautiee…"

"Yes… my Thirst Quencher?"

"I need to tell you something…"

"Okay…"

"Let's get in the car…" he said as he opened the door for her… "I'll tell you on the way home…"

"Okay…" she sighed. Bazil got in the car, started the car, and drove out the parking lot before he spoke…

"Mary went to Planned Parenthood…"

"Oh wow – what was she doing at Planned Parenthood?"

"I don't know…"

"Wait a minute – how do you know Mary was at Planned Parenthood?"

"Chandler told me…"

"Oh – okay…"

"Beautiee…"

"Yes Bazil?"

"There was an explosion at the clinic…"

"Oh my God!"

"Wayne called Chandler because he went to the clinic to pick her up and he couldn't find her…"

"He thought Mary was dead?"

"Yea…"

"Does Starr know all this?"

"No – Chandler said he couldn't tell her…"

"Wait a minute – Starr thought her mother was dead – but doesn't know how she could've been killed?"

"Yea…"

"Bazil – she's gonna ask questions – Chandler has to tell her…"

"I know – but I need to tell you something else…"

"Okay…"

"I called Conrad to see what he could find out…"

"Did he find out anything?"

"Yea…"

"Do I wanna know?"

"I'm not sure…"

"What happened?"

"There's a terrorist group known as the Army of God…"

"Wait – what the fuck – Mary went to the clinic – and it was blown up by terrorists?"

"Yes…"

"So Wayne went to pick her up… and he thought she died in the explosion…"

"Yea…"

"Oh my God – that's horrible!"

"Yea…"

"Why wasn't he with her? Why did he let her go by herself – what the fuck is wrong with him? See – now I'm mad!" Bazil bust out laughing… "What's so fuckin' funny?" Beautiee snapped…

"I'm... I don't know what to say... it's not like she's your best friend..."

"She could've died – and he wasn't there – and he would've had to live with that – you know what – I know what happened – he told her he didn't want the baby and she went to have an abortion – that's why he didn't go with her – mutha fucka – uggh!"

"Beautiee... please... calm down... I'm sorry..."

"No – I'm sorry... I didn't mean to snap at you – I just can't believe that – I'm pregnant – I can only imagine what she went through – I'd be devastated if you told me to have an abortion – but you'd never do that – and you'd never let me go through something like that alone..."

"Damn right I wouldn't..."

"I love you..."

"I love you too..." Bazil said as he took her hand and kissed it...

"Starr... come sit down..." Chandler said as he took her hands, led her to the couch, and they both sat down..."

"I'm scared Chandler..."

"Why?"

"Because... we need to talk..."

"Yes... we do..."

"What's wrong Chandler?" Starr whispered as she started crying...

"Stop that…" he said as he pulled her into a kiss…

"Okay…" she sniffed…

"Your mother went to Planned Parenthood…"

"Because she found out she was pregnant?"

"Yea…"

"I still can't believe it… I'm so happy for Mommy… and Dad…" she sighed…

"Starr… listen to me…"

"Okay…"

"There was an explosion at the clinic…"

"Oh my God…"

"Wayne went to pick your mother up… and he couldn't find her…"

"You mean he thought Mommy was inside?"

"Yea…"

"Why didn't he go with her?"

"I don't know…"

"I don't know what I would've done if Mommy was killed…" Starr whispered as she started crying again…"

"Starr… stop crying… please…" Chandler said as he kissed her…

"Why was there an explosion?"

"There was a bomb…"

"Oh my God! Why?"

"Starr… you know Planned Parenthood is for abortions too… right?"

"Oh my God! Was Mommy trying to have an abortion?"

"Starr – Wayne was so happy when he told us they were having a baby..."

"Yea... he was..."

"Your mother was just there at the wrong time..."

"Why doesn't Mommy have a doctor?"

"Starr?"

"Yes Chandler?"

"Stop it..."

"But Chandler..."

"Star – your mother is alive – she's pregnant – and she's happy – let her have that – she deserves it..."

"You're right Chandler... I'm sorry..." she said as she pulled him into a hug..."

"I'ma let you have that one..."

"C'mon Mary – we need to go..." Wayne said as he opened the door...

"Wayne?"

"Yes Mary?"

"Did you mean what you said?"

"About what?"

"About the baby?"

"Come here Mary..." I walked over to Wayne, he took me in his arms, kissed me, and said, "We're having a baby..."

"We're having a baby..." I cried...

"We need to go now..."

"Where are we going?" I asked as we left the house and went to get in the car...

"I'll explain on the way..." Wayne answered as we went to get in the car.

Chapter 12

"Beautiee – everything alright?" Keisha asked as we dragged ourselves to the front door...

"Girl – what are you doing up so late?" Beautiee asked...

"Hey Troy..." Bazil yawned...

"Y'all good?" Troy asked...

"Girl – I'm tired – come inside..." Beautiee yawned...

"I knew it!" Keisha snapped...

"Knew what?" Bazil asked as he opened the door and they all went inside...

"I knew something was up..." Keisha laughed as they went into the living room and sat down...

"Something's up alright..." Bazil said as he rubbed the back of his head...

"Damn Bazil – what happened?" Troy asked as Bazil went towards the library without answering him... "Damn – he can't even talk about it – it must be bad..." Troy said as Bazil came back with a bottle of Hennessey and two glasses... "Oh shit – I know it's bad now – hurry up!" Troy said...

"I'ma go put Jay to bed – I'll be right back – don't start without me..." Beautiee said as she turned to leave...

"Hurry up dammit!" Keisha laughed. Bazil poured two glasses of Hennessey as Beautiee went upstairs. They both gulped it down and Bazil poured them another one as Beautiee came back into the living room and sat down next to Bazil...

"I got a call from Chandler... he was frantic... he said Starr needed us..."

"Oh shit!" Troy exclaimed...

"At the same time – Jay started screaming – and he wouldn't stop!" Beautiee exclaimed...

"Your son is something else!" Keisha exclaimed...

"We grabbed Jay and flew out the house..." Bazil said...

"Bazil thought Jay was hungry – but the way he was screaming I knew something was wrong with Starr – and here's the kicker..." Beautiee paused...

"What?" Keisha asked...

"Bazil asked Jay if that's why he was crying... and he stopped crying!"

"No he didn't!" Troy exclaimed...

"He did..." Bazil acknowledged... "So we get to Chandler's house – I call him to tell him were downstairs – he tells me hurry up..." Bazil said as he started tearing up...

"Damn Bazil..." Troy said as he started rubbing Bazil's back...

"So we get inside – Starr runs to her father – busts out crying - Bazil's crying – and Jay starts screaming again..." Beautiee said as she's shaking her head...

"What the hell happened?" Keisha snapped...

"Wayne called Chandler – he couldn't find Mary..."

"Wait a minute – Mary's missing?" Keisha asked...

"Actually – it was Sergeant Gallagher that called Chandler..." Bazil said...

"Oh shit! She was kidnapped?" Troy asked...

"They thought she was dead..." Bazil answered...

"No!" Troy gasped...

"Okay wait – I'm confused..." Keisha said...

"I pulled Chandler to the side and asked him what happened – he said Sergeant Gallagher called him because..." Bazil paused, took a deep breath, and sighed... "There was a terrorist attack at Planned Parenthood... and..."

"Wait one muthafuckin' minute!" Keisha interrupted...

"Keisha – let him finish..." Beautiee said...

"There was a terrorist attack at Planned Parenthood... a bomb went off... people were taken out in body bags... Wayne couldn't find Mary... they needed him to go to the morgue to identify the bodies to see if Mary was one of them..."

"See – I have a fuckin' attitude – first of all – what the fuck was she doin' there – second – why the fuck wasn't he with her – uuugghhh – I swear ta God – Troy..."

"Keisha – you already know!" Troy said as he tried to calm her down...

"Is she alright?" Keisha asked...

"I swear – you and Beautiee said the same shit!" Bazil laughed...

"Damn right we did!" Beautiee said as she high-fived Keisha...

"'Cause we're women – and that's that bullshit – is she alright – she better be alright!" Keisha snapped...

"She is Keisha..." Beautiee acknowledged...

"This some funny shit – you like her about as much as Beautiee – and Beautiee can't stand her!" Bazil laughed...

"I'on like her ass – but I'm a woman – and I'm pregnant... and... oh shit – is she pregnant?" Keisha asked...

"Yes girl!" Beautiee acknowledged...

"Wooooow!" Troy exclaimed...

"So – we all pregnant – we need to eat – so I ordered pizza – so we're all eating – Wayne calls

– Chandler puts it on speaker – we're all happy Mary's okay…" Beautiee said…

"All? Who else was there?" Keisha asked…

"Charles and Theresa…"

"Oh – okay…"

"Wayne went to pick Mary up from the clinic – and Mary was home the whole time…" Bazil said…

"Well – I'm glad Mary's okay – but it serves his ass right – he should'a been with her – oooh – if something happened to her – that would'a been his ass!" Keisha snapped…

"I'm glad you're happy about that – she'll be at the baby shower with us…" Beautiee said…

"Awww Damn!" Keisha said…

"I knew it!" Bazil laughed…

"Whatchu know?" Keisha asked…

"I knew you didn't like her!" Bazil laughed…

"I don't like her – I never said I did – but since we all pregnant – I'll be nice – for Starr – but she better not start – I'll curse her ass out – Starr gonna have to get over it…"

"Calm down Keisha…" Troy laughed…

"These two – I swear!" Bazil laughed…

"I can't believe they doin' that shit in Canada!" Troy said…

"What – bombing abortion clinics? They're doing that all over…" Bazil said…

"I wonder who died…" Keisha said…

"Somebody that was getting an abortion..." Beautiee answered...

"Beautiee – le'me ask you something..." Keisha said...

"Yea..." Beautiee answered...

"You think so?" Keisha asked...

"Yea..." Beautiee answered again.

Chapter 12

"Wayne?"

"Yes Mary?" Wayne answered as he started the car and followed behind Sergeant Gallagher...

"Why are we going to the station?"

"There was an explosion at Planned Parenthood..."

"Oh my God!"

"Some people were killed..."

"Oh my God!"

"Sergeant Gallagher needs your help..."

"Oh my God! I can't believe I could'a been killed! Thank God I left when I did! Oh my God... you thought I was dead?"

"I'm sorry..." Wayne whispered as he started crying...

"Oh Wayne... I'm sorry..." I said as I started crying...

"You have nothing to be sorry for..."

"I cried most of the time I was there..."

"I should've been with you..." Wayne cried as he took my hand...

"Everyone was so nice to me... and now... oh my God... that coud've been me... thank you God for saving my life..."

"Thank you God..."

"After I spoke to Carol... I told her I couldn't do it..."

"I'm glad you couldn't do it..."

"Really?"

"I meant what I said Mary... we're having a baby..."

"I can't believe it... I prayed and asked God to help me..."

"So did I..."

"I love you so much..."

"I love you too..."

"Everyone's happy for us..."

"Amazing – isn't it?"

"I'm surprised Beautiee's happy for me..."

"Why wouldn't she be happy for you?"

"Well... to be honest... I was a real Bitch..."

"Yes... you were..."

"Wayne!"

"Yes Mary?"

"Nothing – I just didn't expect you to agree with me!" I laughed...

"I think Beautiee knows that's in the past – besides – you can always apologize when you see her again..."

"I said I was a Bitch – I didn't say I was apologizing..." I laughed...

"So… you're not sorry?"

"Not really…"

"Mary!"

"What? You want me to be honest – right?" I laughed…

"I guess…" he sighed. We rode a bit longer until we got to the station. Wayne got out the car, closed the door, came around to the passenger side, opened the door for me, helped me out, pulled me into a kiss, kissed me hard, held me, and whispered in my ear… "Just so you know… when we're done here… I'm taking you home… I'm gonna love you… spoil you… and fuck the shit outta you… every chance I get… you hear me Mommy?"

"Yes Daddy… Yes…" I breathed…

"Good… let's go…" he commanded as he wrapped his arm around me and we went inside the precinct…

"Thanks for coming Mary – we really need your help…" Sergeant Gallagher said as they followed him down the hallway to another room, went inside, and sat down…

"I feel like I'm under arrest…" I said…

"I'm right here…" Wayne said as he took my hand and squeezed it…

"Okay Mary – I need you to tell me everything that happened from the moment you went into the clinic…" Sergeant Gallagher said…

"I'm not doing that…"

"I don't need to know your personal business – I just need to know who you spoke to - what you saw – etc…"

"Did anybody die?"

"Unfortunately… yes…"

"Oh my God… that could've easily been me…" I whispered as I started tearing up…

"Please don't cry…" Wayne said as he started tearing up…

"You need a minute?" Sergeant Gallagher asked…

"Yea…" I answered…

"Okay – I'll go make us some coffee…" he said as he got up and left us alone in the room…

"I'm sorry…" I whispered…

"I'm the one that needs to apologize – you should've never been there in the first place…" Wayne whispered as he kissed my tears, my mouth, pulled me to him, and held me…

"When Carol explained the process… how the medication would force me to miscarry… I broke down… I told her I couldn't go through with it… I was so sad… I just wanted to run… I wanted to beg you to re-consider…"

"You don't have to beg me to do anything – I love you…"

"I was so scared you'd be angry…"

"I was never angry at you… I would've never forgiven myself if anything happened to you… or our child…"

"Did you just say… our child?"

"Yes Mary… God gave us another chance… he blessed us with another child… we have another chance to be happy… and I almost threw it away…"

"Oh my God… Wayne… I'm so happy…"

"So am I…" Wayne said as Sergeant Gallagher came back into the room with two cups of coffee and placed them on the table…

"I made them both light and sweet – I hope that's alright…"

"That's fine…" we both said in unison…

"Good – I'll be right back…" he said as he left the room again…

"Where's he going now?" I asked…

"Who knows?" Wayne answered…

"Sorry about that – I could only carry two cups at a time – I needed a cup myself," he said as he sat down with a cup of black coffee, a pad, and a pen… "You ready?"

"I guess so…" I answered…

"Okay – you can start anywhere you like…"

"Okay… I walked inside and went up to the receptionist…"

"What was her name?"

"Gina…"

"Okay…"

"Gina gave me a clipboard with some papers to fill out - I took the clipboard and sat down… and I started crying…" I said as Wayne started rubbing my back…

"Did you see anyone else in the waiting area?"

"Yes..."

"Would you be able to identify them if I showed you photographs?"

"I might..."

"Okay – continue..."

"One of the ladies asked me if I was alright... I told her no... and she offered me some tissues... and told me I'd be alright..." I said as I started tearing up again...

"Did you get her name?"

"I didn't ask her her name – but when they called her I got it..."

"Do you remember her name?"

"Sarah Mariani..."

"And she was in the waiting area with you?"

"Yes – until they called her to go in the back..."

"Did you get anybody else's name?"

"No..."

"Okay – continue..."

"Carol come out to the waiting area and called my name, so I got up and followed her to the examination room..."

"Did you go back to the waiting area?"

"No – but Carol did..."

"Uh huh – so you were in the room alone?"

"Yes – Carol went to get me some coffee..."

"Okay – when she came back with your coffee – was she alone?"

"Yes…"

"Okay – after you spoke with Carol – did you speak to anyone else?"

"No…"

"Did you see a doctor?"

"No…"

"What did you do?"

"I told Carol I was going to talk to my husband – and then I left…"

"Did you go back to the waiting area?"

"No…"

"How did you get out the building?"

"I walked out the back door…"

"Oh – so there was a back door?"

"Yes…"

"Was there an alarm on that door?"

"No…"

"Okay – so you went out the back door – did you see anyone outside?"

"I wasn't really paying attention – I'm sorry…"

"That's okay – how did you get home?"

"I called an Uber…"

"How long did you wait?"

"About 5 minutes…"

"I need to see your phone…"

"Why?"

"Uber tracks their drivers, locations, arrival times, etc…"

"Oh my God – you don't think my Uber driver had anything to do with this do you?"

"No – but it will show me what time the Uber driver arrived – that'll help…"

"Okay – here…" I said as I handed Sergeant Gallagher my cell phone…

"Thanks…" he said as he started looking through my phone… "Okay – here it is…" he said as he started writing something down on his pad and then he gave me back my phone…

"Thank you…"

"You're welcome – I'm going to show you some photos – let me know who you recognize…"

"Okay…" I said as he opened a folder and spread out the photos so I could look at them… "That's Gina…"

"Okay…" he said as he put her name on a post it, put it on the picture, and moved it to the side…

"That's Carol…"

"Okay…" he said as he put her name on a post it, put it on the picture, and moved it to the side…

"That's Sarah…" I said as I started tearing up…

"Okay…" he said as he put her name on a post it, put it on the picture, and moved it to the side. I looked at the rest of the pictures, but I didn't recognize anyone else… and then I remembered something…

"She was in the waiting room too..." I said as I pointed to the picture...

"Okay – did you get her name?"

"No..."

"Okay – thank you – this helps a lot..."

"I didn't really do anything..."

"Mary – shortly after you left – Gina got an anonymous call – the caller told her there was a bomb and they had 5 minutes to get out..."

"Oh my God! Why?"

"They used to just petition outside in front of the building and harass people going inside – now they've moved on to terrorists that call themselves the Army of God..."

"God doesn't tell them to do that!" I snapped...

"You know that – and I know that – but it doesn't matter – all that matters is that they stop doctors from performing abortions..." he sighed...

"What about the pre-natal care they offer to women that don't have insurance? What about the prevention of STD's? What about the free cancer screenings? What about the free mammograms? Planned Parenthood does a lot more than abortions!" I snapped...

"As far as the Army of God is concerned – none of that matters..."

"How can they call themselves the Army of God and then turn around and commit murder?"

"They believe God gives them permission to use violence to end abortions..." he sighed...

"Thank you God for saving our lives..." I said as I rubbed my stomach...

"Amen to that..." Wayne said as he rubbed my stomach and kissed me...

"You're pregnant?" Sergeant Gallagher asked...

"Yes... she's pregnant..." Wayne beamed...

"Congratulations..."

"Thank you..." we both said in unison...

"I wish everybody could have a happy ending – but unfortunately – I need to go down to the morgue – I need to see if we can identify anyone – and then we need to notify the families..." he said as he got up, picked up the folder with the photos, the note pad, and left the room... and Wayne burst into tears...

"Wayne... I'm right here..." I whispered as I held him and let him cry on my shoulder...

"I... couldn't..."

"Ssshhh..."

"When we got home... Officer Johnson... drove... my car..." he heaved as he continued crying...

"I'm here..." I whispered as I held him and let him cry..."

"He told me... he needed... me... to go... with... him... to the morgue..."

"Wayne... look at me..." I said as I picked up his face with my hands and kissed his tears..."

"I'm sorry..."

"I know..."

"Can you forgive me?"

"Yes... under one condition..."

"Name it..."

"You said something about loving me..." I breathed as I kissed him...

"Yes Mommy..."

"Spoiling me..." I breathed as I kissed him again..."

"Yes Mommy..."

"And... fucking the shit outta me..." I breathed as I let go of Wayne and stood up...

"You ready Mommy?"

"Yes Daddy... I'm ready..." I sighed. Wayne stood up beside me, pushed me back against the wall, pushed his tongue in my mouth, and we tongued each other down for a few minutes...

"Let's go home..." he said as he stopped kissing me, took me by the hand, and pulled me out the door.

Chapter 13

"I thought we were going home..." I said after I noticed he drove in the opposite direction...

"We are..." Wayne answered, looking straight ahead...

"Home's back there..."

"I know..." he said as he took my hand and kissed it. I didn't ask any more questions. I just sighed, smiled, and looked out the window. I didn't give a damn where we were going – all I knew was I was with my husband, we're having a baby, and he's as happy about it as I am...

"Baton Rouge Steakhouse & Bar... hmmm..." I said as we pulled into the parking lot...

"I hope you're hungry..." he said as he parked the car and then got out. Before I could answer him, he came around to the passenger side, opened the door for me, helped me out, pulled me into a kiss, and kissed me hard...

"Mmmm... I could get used to this..."

"Glad to hear it..." he said as he wrapped his arm around me and escorted me inside...

"Welcome to Baton Rouge Steakhouse – follow me…" the hostess said as she picked up two menus and we followed her to a booth… "Take your time – the waitress will be right with you…" she said and then she went back to the front…

"Let's split a Louisiana Chicken Salad…" Wayne said…

"Hmmm… freshly marinated & flame-grilled sliced chicken, Thai peanut sauce, mixed greens, crispy noodles, pineapple-soy dressing – okay – sounds good…" I said…

"I'll have a Baton Rouge Burger…"

"I could've guessed that…" I laughed… "Ground chuck, smoked bacon, Monterey jack cheese, lettuce, tomatoes, onions, Dijonnaise sauce – damn – that sounds delicious – I might get one too!"

"Are you sure?"

"Why?"

"Take a look at their pasta…"

"Ooohhhh…. Seafood Linguine with sautéed jumbo black tiger shrimp, North Atlantic scallops, white wine, rosé sauce – Creamy Spinach & Chicken Penne – freshly marinated & Flame-grilled chicken breast, mushrooms, diced tomatoes, onions, creamy spinach & cheese sauce – nope – I want the baton Rouge Burger!" I laughed… "And I'll have the Apple Cobbler for dessert!"

"Apple Cobbler?"

"Yea…"

"Hmmm – warm apple cobbler with a touch of cinnamon and brown sugar on a layer of rich caramel sauce, sprinkled with walnuts and topped with French vanilla ice cream… yea… I want that too…"

"Have you decided what you want?" the waitress asked as she came over to the table…

"Yes we have…" Wayne answered…

"Okay – tell me what you'd like…" she said…

"We're gonna split the Louisiana Chicken Salad, we'll both have the Baton Rouge Burger, and we'll both have the apple cobbler for dessert…" Wayne said…

"Okay – nice and easy – what can I get you to drink – we have delicious cocktails – and we can make any cocktail alcohol free if you prefer…"

"I'll just have a ginger ale…" I said…

"Same here…" Wayne said…

"Okay – I'll be back…" she said as she went to get our drinks…

"Where'd you find out about this place?" I asked as the waitress placed our drinks on the table…

"I just googled restaurants near me…" he laughed…

"You'll be easy to please…" I laughed…

"What's that supposed to mean?"

"Most men want full-course meals – steak, potatoes, salad – you just want a good burger..."

"Among other things..." he said as he smiled at me mischievously...

"Here's your salad..." the waitress said as she put the salad on the table along with two plates...

"Thanks..." I said as she walked away...

"Looks delicious..." Wayne said as he put some on my plate and then his...

"Oh my God – it's good!" I exclaimed. We finished the salad without speaking until she brought the burgers to the table... "Oh my God – these are huge!" I laughed...

"They're man-sized..." Wayne laughed...

"Can I get you refills on your drinks?" the waitress asked...

"No thanks – I need room for this..." I said as I picked up my burger to take a bite...

"How 'bout you sir?"

"No thanks..." Wayne answered as he picked up his burger and bit into it... "Mmmm... he moaned... and I started getting turned on...

"I can see you're really enjoying that..."

"I am..."

"We haven't had a bad burger yet..."

"No... we haven't..."

"I can't wait to get home..."

"Neither can I..." he breathed...

"Wayne... stop that..." I giggled...

"What am I doing?"

"You know exactly what you're doing..." I laughed...

"I have no idea what you're talking about..." he said as he started rubbing my knee under the table...

"Don't start..." I laughed...

"How we doin' over here?" the waitress asked as she walked up to the table...

"Oh my goodness – you're just about ready for dessert..." she said...

"Yes... we are..." Wayne acknowledged as he moved his hand up my thigh...

"Yea... we're ready..." I said...

"Okay – I'll just take this outta your way and then I'll get your apple cobblers..." she said as she cleaned the table. Wayne moved his hand up to my waist and I jumped when he put his hand in my pants...

"Ohh!"

"You okay?" the waitress asked...

"Yes – I just felt the baby move..." I lied...

"You're pregnant? Congratulations!"

"Thank you..." I beamed...

"I'll be back with your apple cobblers..." she said as she walked away with the dishes...

"You felt the baby move huh?" Wayne laughed...

"Well – I definitely felt something!" I laughed...

"Here's your apple cobblers..." the waitress said as she put the bowls on the table...

"Oh my God!" I exclaimed as I tasted it... "Wayne – promise me you'll bring me back here for dessert..." I said as I ate...

"You got it..." he said as he ate...

"Excuse me – could you turn that up?" I asked the waitress as she turned up the television...

"This is Ken Shaw, CTV News. We interrupt our regularly scheduled programming to bring you this update – earlier this week our reporter, Tracy Tong, was at Planned Parenthood where a terrorist attack took place. According to an eye-witness, a member of the Army of God made an anonymous phone call letting them know there was a bomb in the building and they had 5 minutes to get out..." I could see Gina on camera crying as she spoke to the reporter and Wayne came over next to me and held me as I started crying...

"Thank God she made it out..." I whispered as the anchorman continued...

"Several people were taken to the hospital for injuries; however, there were also come causalitics..."

"Oh my God..." I whispered as I saw the fire department, the FBI, the bomb squad, and the body bags... "Look – Sergeant Gallagher..." I whispered as I continued crying... and then I saw Wayne... "Wayne..." I whispered...

"They wouldn't let me through..." he said as he started tearing up...

"At this time we're able to confirm that Dr. Berkley was killed in the explosion..." the anchorman said as they put up his picture...

"He was loved by everyone..." Carol said as they interviewed her...

"That's Carol..." I said as I pointed to the television...

"Sarah Mariani was also killed in the explosion..." the anchorman said...

"Oh my God... Sarah..." I cried...

"Mary... I'm sorry..." Wayne whispered as he held me...

"I wanna go home..." I cried as I pushed the apple cobbler away...

"Oh my God – what happened?" the waitress asked as she came over to the table...

"She just found out her friend was killed..." Wayne answered...

"Oh my God – I'm sorry – don't worry about the check..." she said...

"I'll pay the check..." Wayne said...

"It's okay – I'll let the manager know..."

"Thanks – but I'm leaving a tip – and I won't take no for an answer..."

"Okay – thanks – I hope we see you again..."

"You will – c'mon Mary – let's go..." he said as he helped me up, wrapped his arm around me, and led me out the door. When we started walking towards another store away from the car I tried to stop him...

"Wayne... please... I just want to go home..."

"Mary – I know you want to go home – I'll take you home – I have a surprise for you..."

"You do?"

"Yes..."

"Okay..." I sighed as we walked a bit further... "Lazy Boy? We're going shopping?" I asked as we got closer to the store...

"Yea..."

"Perfect – just what I need..." I breathed as we went inside...

"Welcome to Lazy Boy – my name is Raymond – how can I help you?"

"Hello Raymond – I'm here to keep a promise I made to my wife..." Wayne answered...

"Okay! I can definitely help you with that! Where would you like to start?"

"I'd like to start with the Hadleigh Rice Carved King Bed..."

"Oh Wayne! You remembered!" I exclaimed...

"Of course I remembered..." he said as he pulled me into a kiss...

"Do you have an account with us?" Raymond asked...

"I will as soon as you process my application..." Wayne answered...

"Okay – I'll get right on that – I just need..."

"Here…" Wayne interrupted as he handed him his driver's license and a credit card…

"Okay – I'll be right back – in the meantime – please look around – the bed you want is on display over there…" he said as he pointed towards the back of the store…

'Oh Wayne – they have the whole set – it's beautiful!" I exclaimed as I hurried toward the back of the store…

"Lord – please help me – I just want her to be happy…" Wayne prayed out loud…

"I know…" God answered…

"Mr. Robinson – your application's been approved…" Raymond beamed as he went over to Wayne…

"Thank you – what's my limit?" Raymond walked over to Wayne and whispered in his ear… "$7,000…"

"Okay – thanks…" Wayne said as he walked over to me…

"Can we get the bed?" I asked…

"We can get the whole set…"

"We can? Oh Wayne!" I exclaimed as I hugged him…

"We can have everything delivered and set up for you today – if you're willing to take the floor sample…" Raymond said…

"We'll take it…" Wayne said…

"How's ten percent off sound?" Raymond asked…

"Can you do a little better?" Wayne asked...

"Le'me see what I can do..." Raymond said as he went inside the office...

"Let me guess – he wants a discount – and ten percent isn't good enough – right?" Raymond's manager asked sarcastically...

"Yea..." Raymond answered...

"I swear – I'm so sick of these people that come in here and expect something for nothing – that shit gets on my fuckin' nerves..."

"Sir – he's buying the Hadleigh Rice Carved King Bed – and he's buying the complete set..." Raymond interrupted...

"Did you say he's buying the complete set?"

"Yea..." Raymond beamed... "and he's willing to take the floor sample..."

"Damn – he must have excellent credit!"

"He does..."

"Let's see – that's a little over $5,000 – tell him we'll waive the delivery fee – I'm sure he'll want a mattress and box spring – pillows – a bed set – what size is he buying?"

"King size..."

"Oh yea – we'll definitely waive the delivery fee..." the manager beamed...

"Okay – ten percent discount - and we're waiving the delivery fee – right?"

"Right..."

"Okay – thanks!" Raymond exclaimed as he came running out... "Mr. Robinson – as I said earlier – we'll give you a ten percent discount – and we'll waive the delivery fee – how's that?"

"How's that sound to you Dear?" Wayne asked…

"Sounds like we can use that ten percent to get a new mattress to go with our new bedroom set…" I answered…

"Okay – Mr. Robinson – if you'll just sign here – we'll get this out to you later today…" Raymond said as he handed Wayne the application and a pen…

"I'll sign it… after I read it…" Wayne said as he sat down at a table and went over the application and the receipt… "It says here we're getting two twin box springs…"

"Yes – most of the time we can't get the king-size box spring through the door so we use two twin box springs – this way we don't have any issues – and we don't disappoint our customers – I took the liberty of ordering you the pillowtop mattress – I hope that's alright – I can adjust it if you like…" Raymond answered…

"We'll go with the pillowtop…" I sighed…

"Okay – thank you Raymond…" Wayne said as he signed the application and the receipt…

"Will you be needing any furniture for the living room?" Raymond asked…

"Actually – now that you mention it – we do need furniture for the living room – but we can't do that until we get our new floor installed..." Wayne answered...

"Oh okay – make sure you add your email to the application – this way you'll get our offers..."

"Okay..." Wayne said as he added his email and then he handed Raymond the application...

"Thank you – and welcome to Lazy Boy – you'll have your furniture in a few hours..."

"Thank you Raymond - you ready Mary?" he said as he looked at me mischievously...

"Yes... I'm ready..."

"Let's go home..." he said as he came towards me, wrapped his arm around me, and led me out the store...

"Damn – how the hell did that White man pull that fine sistah?" Raymond asked out loud...

"Happens all the time..." the manager sighed...

"That's alright – my Queen is out there..." Raymond said as Rhonda walked in... "Hello Beautiful..." Raymond said as he went over to her... "My name is Raymond... what can I do for you today?" he asked as he smiled...

"Thank you for the compliment – you can start by letting me know what time you get off work..." she answered...

"I can clock out right now and take you to lunch – if you're hungry..." he answered with a smile...

"Oh I'm hungry alright – how 'bout you help me buy a living room set – and then you give me your phone number – and then I'll call you and let you know what time I'll be ready for you to take me out to dinner…" she answered…

"Here – take my card – my cell number's at the bottom…" he said excitedly…

"Thank you Raymond…" she said as she smiled and put the card in her pocket… "Now – let's see what we can do about getting me some furniture and make sure it's comfortable – and sturdy – I need to make sure my man's comfortable when he comes by my place…" she said…

"Did you just say… your man?" Raymond asked as he smiled at her mischievously…

"Yes… I said my man…" she answered…

"Umm… okay… we have something over here I think you'll like…" he said as he took her over to the sectionals.

Chapter 14

"Are you ready Mrs. Robinson?" Wayne asked after parking the car and turning off the ignition...

"Yes Mr. Robinson... I'm ready..." I sighed. Wayne got out, came over to the passenger side, opened the door for me, helped me out the car, pulled me into a kiss... and then I saw it... "Wayne – look!"

"Oh wow – c'mon..." he said as he pulled me to the front door...

"Mr. Robinson?"

"Yes – I'm Mr. Robinson..." Wayne answered...

"We're glad you're home – I didn't want to take this delivery back..." the deliveryman said...

"Even if I wasn't here – I'da been here..." Wayne said...

"We go through that a lot..." the deliveryman said...

"Really?"

"You'd be surprised – and then they have the nerve to get mad at us when we tell them we need to reschedule..."

"My wife wouldn't stand for that..." Wayne laughed... "Let me open the door for you..."

"Hello Mrs. Robinson – let us know what room you'd like us to set everything up in – okay?" the deliveryman asked me...

"Okay..." I said as I went inside and waited for them. The deliverymen started bringing everything in and things were going smoothly until the first deliveryman called out...

"Mr. Robinson?"

"I'll be right there..." Wayne said as he went down the hall to the master bedroom... "Looks good..." Wayne said as he looked at the bed...

"I'm glad you're happy – but unfortunately, we can't fit the rest of the furniture in here..."

"Mary – c'mere a sec..." Wayne said. I went down the hall and looked in the room...

"Oooohhh... it looks nice!" I exclaimed...

"I'm glad you like it – but we can't fit the rest of the furniture in here..." Wayne said...

"We can put the TV stand on that wall – we'll put a nightstand on each side of the bed – and we'll put the other pieces in the 2nd bedroom..." I said...

"Sounds good..." Wayne said...

"Long as we don't have to take this back – we'll put it anywhere you want..." the 1st deliveryman laughed... "Aiight guys – you heard the lady – let's git it!"

"Aiight man!" the 2nd and 3rd deliverymen yelled from the living room...

"I can't wait to keep my promise to you..." Wayne breathed in my ear as he pulled me to him...

"I can't wait for you to keep it..." I whispered back. We watched as the deliverymen worked getting the rest of the furniture in the 2nd bedroom and setting it up...

"Okay! We're done!" the 1st deliveryman said...

"Looks good..." Wayne said... "Mary – everything look okay?" I looked around at the furniture and then I looked back at Wayne...

"Everything looks fine..." I sighed...

"Okay! If you'll just sign here – we'll be outta your way..." the 1st deliveryman said as he handed Wayne the paper and a pen. Wayne stood there for a few moments, read over the paper, and signed it... "Thank you Mr. Robinson – enjoy your bedroom – have a great day..." the 1st deliveryman said as he put the paper in his pocket along with the pen...

"Have a nice day..." the 2nd and 3rd deliverymen said as they followed the 1st deliveryman out the door...

"Come with me Mommy..." Wayne said as he took me by the hand and led me into the bedroom...

"Yes Daddy?" I asked...

"Help me take the plastic off this mattress…"

"Yes Daddy…" I said as we started taking the plastic off the mattress. Once we had all the plastic off the mattress, Wayne opened the bed-in-a-bag, took out the sheets, the skirt, the pillow cases, and the comforter, and put them in the middle of the bed…

"We'll do this together…" he said as he unfolded the skirt…"

"Okay Daddy…"

"Left up your end of the mattress…" I lifted up my end of the mattress and he put the skirt on the box spring. I dropped my end of the mattress and Wayne picked up his end, put the skirt on the box spring, and dropped the mattress back down… "Okay – you pull the sheet up on your side and I'll pull it up on my side…"

"Yes Daddy…" I said as we both pulled the sheet attached to the skirt up…

"Come here Mommy…" I went over to Wayne and stood in front of him…

"Yes Daddy?" Wayne pulled me to him, kissed me, and grabbed my ass… 'Mmmm…" I moaned in his mouth…

"Let's put the sheets on…"

"Okay Daddy…" I said as he let me go, picked up the fitted sheet, and unfolded it. After we put it on the bed we unfolded the top sheet, put it on the bed, and then we put the pillow cases on the pillows…

"Now for the comforter..." he said. After we put the comforter on the bed he came over to me and started undressing me. He pulled my shirt over my head and kissed me as he put his arms around me and unhooked my bra... "Your breasts are so soft..." he breathed as he massaged them and sucked on them...

"Mmmm... that feels good..." I moaned. He kissed his way down my stomach, got down on his knees, and held me by my hips as he spoke...

"Hi Baby..." he said as he continued kissing my stomach... "I'm your Daddy..." he said as he kissed my stomach again... "And I love you..."

"Oh Wayne..." I whispered as he slid my pants along with my panties off my ass and down to the floor. Wayne stood up, kissed me, picked me up in his arms, carried me over to the bed, and laid me down on the bed. I watched as he took off his clothes, deliberately taking his time...

"You want me Mommy?"

"Yes Daddy... yes..." I breathed. Wayne got on the bed on his knees...

"Get up on your knees..."

"Yes Daddy..." I squealed as I got up on my knees...

"Turn around..." I turned around as I was told and closed my eyes. Wayne came up behind me, pulled me to him, and I could feel his dick against my ass as he began kissing me on my neck...

"Ooohhh..." I moaned...

"Mommy..." he whispered in my ear...

"Yes Daddy..." I whispered...

"Tell Daddy what you want..."

"I want you..." I moaned..."

"Where?" he breathed as he ran his hands up and down my body...

"Everywhere..." I breathed...

"So... should I start here?" he breathed as he put his hand between my legs and started playing with my clit...

"Yes... yes..." I moaned. Wayne eased himself in my ass and I gasped... "Oh Daddy..." I moaned...

"Yes Mommy..." Wayne breathed in my ear as he fucked my ass while simultaneously playing with my clit...

"Huh... huh... huh..."

"You like that Mommy?" h breathed as he continued fucking my ass and playing with my clit...

"Yes Daddy... yes... huh... fuck me Daddy..." I moaned as I moved my hands up behind his head and leaned back against him...

"You ready to cum for Daddy?" he breathed...

"Yes Daddy! Yes! Fuck me! I'm cumming! I'm cumming!" Wayne continued fucking my ass and playing with my clit as I came so hard my body trembled down to my knees...

"Get on your back Mommy..."

"Yes Daddy..." I breathed as I laid down on my back. Wayne looked down at me and sucked my juices off his fingers...

"Spread your legs..."

"Yes Daddy..." I breathed as I spread my legs and Wayne got down between them...

"Waaayyynnneee!" I moaned as he licked, slurped, and sucked on my pussy...

"Mmmm..." Wayne moaned as he continued licking, slurping, and sucking...

"Huh... Huh... Huh... Huh..." I grabbed his head and fucked his face as I started cumming again... "Wayne... don't stop... don't stop... that's it... right there... Fuuccckkk!" Wayne continued licking, slurping, and sucking as I arched my back, came up off the bed, and fell back down... "Wayne... wait..."

"No..." he said and then went back to devouring me...

"Wayne... it's sensitive..." Wayne continued licking, slurping, and sucking softly until his thirst was quenched... and then he came up from between my legs, laid down on top of me, and eased himself inside me as he pushed his tongue in my mouth...

"Mmmmm..... Mmmmm.... Mmmmm... Mmmmm..." Wayne was fucking me hard, hitting my spot, and I was in heaven...

"Mmmph! Mmmph! Mmmph! Mmmph!..."

"Mmmmm….. Mmmmm…. Mmmmm… Mmmmm…"

"Mmmph! Mmmph! Mmmph! Mmmph!..."

"Mmmmm….. Mmmmm…. Mmmmm… Mmmmm…MMMMM

"Mmmph! Mmmph! Mmmph! Mmmph!... MMMPH!" Wayne collapsed on top of me and continued kissing me for a few moments…

"Daddy…" I breathed…

"Yes Mommy…" he breathed between kisses…

"You kept… your… promise…"

"Which one…"

"You fucked… the shit… outta me…"

"I did…"

"Do it again…"

"I will…"

"You promise?"

"I promise… but we need to talk…" he said as he laid down beside me and propped himself up on his elbow…

"Okay…" I sighed…

"I wanna talk… about the baby…"

"Okay…"

"Let's pick out names…"

"Wayne… you wanna do that… now?"

"Yea…"

"Okay… our son will be named after you…"

"Me?"

"Yes…"

"Are you sure?"

"Yes... I'm sure..."

"I'd like that... but..."

"But what?"

"What if we have a girl?"

"If we have a girl... I want her name to be Sky..."

"Hmmm... Starr... and Sky..."

"How does that sound?"

"Sounds beautiful..."

"You really think so?"

"Yes..." he breathed and then he kissed me... "Because..." he breathed as he kissed me again... "Every night..." he breathed as he kissed me again... "When we look up..." he breathed as he kissed me again... "We'll be reminded..." he breathed as he kissed me again... "Of our children..."

"Wayne..." I whispered as I started to cry... "I love you so much..."

"I love you too..." he breathed as he kissed me again... and then he got on top of me... "Now..." he breathed as he eased himself inside me and started thrusting... "I made you a promise..." he breathed as he lifted my legs, spread them, and fucked me deeper...

"Wayne... oh God... yes..."

Chapter 15

"Oh my God... was I drinking?" I asked out loud as I felt my head throbbing...

"Bang! Bang! Bang! Bang!"

"What the hell is he doing?" I asked as I got up, put on my robe, and went towards the living room... "Wayne?"

"Did I wake you?" he asked as he took a break, put down the mallet, and wiped sweat from his head...

"How long have you been out here?"

"About 2 hours..."

"How long have you been banging on the floor?"

"About 10 minutes..."

"Yea... you woke me..." I yawned. Wayne got up from the floor, came over to me, and pulled me into a kiss...

"I'm sorry... I wanted to surprise you..."

"Another surprise? You are a man of your word – be careful though – you keep spoiling me like this I could get used to it..." I laughed...

"Come sit down – I'll get us some coffee…" he said as he took me by the hand, led me to the table, and pulled out the chair for me…

"Thank you Baby…"

"You're welcome…" he said as he reached up in the cabinet, took down two mugs, made us both coffee, came to the table, and sat down with me…

"So…" I said as I sipped my coffee… "You said you had a surprise for me…" Wayne bust out laughing…

"What's so funny?"

"Look at the floor…" he answered as he sipped his coffee…

"Oh Wayne! It's beautiful! How did you…"

"I pulled up the carpet – I went out – I bought the floor – I put it in myself…"

"I love it…"

"I love you…"

"I love you too…"

"We need to go shopping again today…"

"Wayne – I love shopping – but I was hoping we could spend the day together… in bed…" I sighed…

"I'd love to spend the day in bed with you – but I start work next week – and I need to make sure everything's taken care of so you can relax…"

"Wayne – you can take a minute…" I laughed…

"I could – but I'm not…" he laughed…

"Okay – we can go shopping if you want – where are we going?"

"We're going back to Lazy Boy…"

"We are?"

"Yea…"

"Okay – and then where are we going?"

"We're going to Target…"

"Good – 'cause we need an iron, an ironing board, and garbage cans…"

"Okay…" he sighed…

"You had something else in mind?"

"Flat screens…"

"Oh my God – you're right – we don't have a television!" I laughed…

"After we get back we need to put in a call to Dish TV…"

"Dish TV?"

"That's the best option out here…."

"Okay…" I sighed…

"Don't worry – I'll make sure we have all your favorite channels…"

"And the NBA and the NFL packages…"

"I don't think we need to get the sports package – Dish has a great sports channel for NBA and NFL…"

"Okay – I guess I'll get ready…" I said as I stood up from the table and started to go towards the bathroom…

"Wait…" he said as he took my hand… "I'll come with you…"

"Okay…" I laughed as he held me against him and walked me backwards into the bathroom… and then he stood there looking around with his hand under his chin… "Wayne?"

"Yea…" he answered… still thinking…

"What are you doing?"

"I'm thinking…"

"About what?"

"Do you remember what you said to me before we got the first house?"

"I said a lot of things…" I laughed…

"Let me refresh your memory…" he said as he came up behind me, pulled me against him, and started kissing my neck…

"Oohhh… I'm not sure… I may have said something…"

"Do you remember our wedding night?" he whispered in my ear…

"Yeesss…" I moaned…

"Do you remember when we took out first shower together?"

"Yesss…" I moaned…

"Do you remember what you said…"

"Yccsss…"

"Tell me…" he breathed as he opened my robe, slid it off my shoulders, and turned me around…

"I said… I hope there's a bench in the shower…" I breathed…

"What else did you say?" he breathed as he pulled me closer and held me against him…

"I said I hope there's a bench in the shower... so I could suck you upside-down... and you can fuck me right-side up..." I breathed...

"Turn around..." Wayne said as he turned me around...

"Okay..."

"What do you see?"

"Oh Wayne... are you telling me..."

"Yes Mary..." he said as he turned me back around and pulled me to him again... "We're getting a new bathroom..."

"A walk-in shower... with a bench?"

"Yea..."

"We need a tub... for the baby..."

"We have a tub in the other bathroom..." he said and then he pulled me into a kiss...

"You're right..." I said as I kissed him back...

"Let's get ready and get outta here – otherwise we won't leave at all..."

"That's fine with me..."

"Mary..."

"Okay, okay – I'll let you spoil me rotten – how's that?" I laughed...

"I'll spoil you until the baby comes... and then I'll spoil both of you..." he said as he kissed me again...

"I love you..."

"I love you too... I'm going to get our clothes together while you're in the shower..." he said as he turned to leave...

"Wayne... wait..."

"Yes Mary?"

"I thought you wanted to come with me?"

"I'll come with you... after we get back..." he laughed as he left me in the bathroom. I took a quick shower, brushed my teeth, and got out... and then I called Wayne...

"Honey?"

"I'll be right there..." he said and then he came in the bathroom... and I pulled him into a hug and started kissing him... "Mary... wait..."

"I don't wanna..." I whined...

"Mary..." he said between kisses... I love you..."

"I love you too..."

"I need you to go get dressed..."

"Okay..." I sighed. Wayne pulled me back into a kiss and then he said... "I'll make it up to you... I promise..."

"Okay..." I sighed and then I left to get dressed. I heard the water go on and Wayne started singing as I was getting dressed... "Thank you Lord..." I sighed...

"You're welcome..." he answered. Wayne came into the bedroom and I dropped to my knees and started kissing his dick...

"Mary..." he whispered...

"Yes Daddy?" I answered before taking his dick in my mouth. Wayne didn't bother resisting – he grabbed my head, played with my hair, and let me suck his dick...

"Mmmm.... Shit... that's it Mommy... suck it..." I took his dick all the way in my mouth, moved my hands up, and grabbed his ass while I continued deep throating him...

"Fuck... I'm cumming!" Wayne growled as his legs shook. Wayne came in my mouth and I held onto his ass to keep his dick in my mouth as I swallowed every drop and continued sucking... "Mary... wait..."

"Mmmm mmmm..." I moaned as I shook my head no and continued sucking...

"Mary... easy... it's sensitive..." I let go of his ass, took my mouth off his dick, and looked up at him... "Come here..." he breathed...

"Yes Daddy?" I said as I stood up in front of him. Wayne pulled me into a kiss, held me, and whispered in my ear...

"When we get back home... I'm going to return the favor..."

"Can you return the favor now Daddy? Please?"

"No..." he answered and then he stepped back away from me, smiling mischievously as he started getting dressed...

"Okay... I'll wait..." I sighed. I watched Wayne get dressed and when he was finished, he pulled me to him again – but this time he slid his hand in my pants and started playing with my pussy... "Wayne..." I whispered...

"Yes... that's it... this is how I want it..." he breathed and then he took his hand out my pants...

"Wayne... why'd you stop?"

"I like torturing you..." he answered. I started to pout so he took me by the hand and led me out the house to the car...

"Where are we going first?" I asked...

"I'm taking you to breakfast..."

"Okay..." I sighed. Wayne drove for a bit and I relaxed and looked out the window. I started smiling to myself and Wayne took my hand as he continued driving until we arrived...

"We're here..." he said as he pulled into the parking lot...

"Hmmm – Eggsmart – I like that!" I beamed. We got out the car and went inside...

"Good morning – welcome to Eggsmart – have a seat anywhere you like – I'll be right with you..." the waitress said as she went to get meus...

"I like this restaurant already..." I said...

"Me too..." Wayne said...

"Here's our menu..." the waitress said as she put the menus on the table... "Can I get you some coffee?"

"Yes please..." Wayne answered...

"Okay – I'll be right back..."

"I already know what I want..." I said...

"So do I..." Wayne said. The waitress came back with a pot of coffee and set it in the middle of the table with two cups, flavored creamers, sugar, and spoons...

"What can I getcha?" she asked...

"I'll have the Eggsmart classic breakfast..." I answered...

"Okay – will that be with sausage, bacon, or turkey bacon?"

"Turkey bacon..."

"Okay – what can I get you sir?" she asked Wayne...

"I'll have the New York Striploin & eggs..."

"Got it..." she said and then she went to walk away but I stopped her...

"Excuse me..."

"Yes Maam?"

"Can we have our eggs scrambled?"

"Yes Maam – we serve all our guests scrambled eggs – unless they request something different..."

"Okay – thanks..."

"You're welcome..." she said as she walked away...

"Let me make your coffee..." Wayne said as he picked up the pot, poured us coffee, and then added the creamer and sugar...

"Mmm... this coffee is good..." I moaned...

"Don't start..." Wayne laughed...

"What'd I say?" I laughed. We finished our coffee just as the waitress was bringing our plates... "Ooohhh... this looks delicious!" I beamed...

"Wait 'till you taste it..." the waitress said as she put the plates down on the table and Wayne smiled at me mischievously...

"Don't start!" I laughed...

"Enjoy your breakfast – if you need anything at all – let me know..." the waitress said before walking over to another table...

"This is as delicious as it looks..." Wayne said after trying the steak...

"Mmmm.... You're right..." I agreed after tasting my turkey bacon. Wayne poured us some more coffee, added the creamer and sugar, and we drank more coffee while eating... "I wanna come back here..." I said...

"We can come back here this weekend if you want..."

"They might want you to work this weekend..."

"Right now my schedule is Monday through Friday..."

"Oh wow – that's good..."

"I may ask them to put me on Saturdays..."

"You wanna work six days a week?" I whined...

"I wanna pay these bills off asap – and then we can start saving money for the baby..."

"I love you so much..." I sighed as I took his hand...

"I love you too..."

"You don't have to work so hard..."

"Yes... I do... for now..."

"Wayne... I need you..."

"Mary... I'm here..."

"That's not what I mean..." I sighed...

"Mary..." he said as he took my hand and kissed it... "I won't overdo it... I promise..."

"I just want you home..."

"I'll come home after work... and I won't work on Saturdays... if that's what you want..."

"Thank you..."

"You don't have to thank me..." he said as he leaned over the table and kissed me...

"How was everything?" the waitress asked as she came over to the table...

"Delicious..." Wayne answered...

"Glad to hear that – can I get you anything else?"

"No thanks..." Wayne answered...

"Alrighty – here's your check – you can pay at the register whenever you're ready..." she said as she placed the check on the table and then went to another table...

"C'mon – let's go..." Wayne said as he stood up and stretched out his hand to take mine...

'Okay!" I squealed as I put my hand in his, he helped me up out of the booth, and we went to the register to pay the check. After we paid the check we went outside and walked to Lazy Boy..."

"Hey! Welcome back!" Raymond exclaimed as we walked in...

"Hello Raymond..." Wayne said...

"How's the bedroom?"

"It's wonderful…" I sighed…

"That's nice…" Raymond said…

"It certainly is…" Wayne agreed as he looked at Raymond and smiled mischievously…

"So what can I do for you today?"

"We're here to get living room furniture…" I answered…

"Nice! Are you looking for Family, Comfortable, Classic, or Modern?"

"We're definitely not looking for modern…" Wayne laughed…

"I don't want classic either – I want to sit on my furniture – not showcase it…" I laughed…

"Showcase it?" Raymond asked…

"I had a girlfriend that had a classic living room – it was gorgeous – but she never let her children go in the living room – and when I went to visit her – we couldn't eat or drink in there – we always had to stay in the kitchen!" I laughed… "What's the point of having a living room if you're not going to live in it?" I laughed again…

"I have just what you're looking for – come with me…" Raymond said as we followed him over to the area with different sectionals…

"Ohhh… I like this one!" I squealed…

"The Collins Sectional – that's one of our best sellers…" Raymond said…

"Oh wow…" Wayne said as he sat down… "Mary – come sit with me…"

"Okay…" I said as I sat down beside him and he put his arm around me… "Mmmm…. I could definitely get used to this…" I said…

"That set includes a sleeper… and an ottoman…" Raymond said…

"We might as well get the sleeper – we don't have a guest room anymore – the twins can sleep in the room with the baby but Chandler and Starr will need a place to sleep…" Wayne said…

"You're having twins? Congratulations!" Raymond exclaimed…

"Thank you – but my daughter's the one having twins…" I said… "We're just having one baby…"

"Mary? Is that you?" she asked as she walked in and came towards us…

"Hey Babe…" Raymond said as he kissed her…

"Rhonda!" I exclaimed as I jumped up off the sectional, went over to her, and we hugged each other…

"Hey girl! Hi Wayne…" she said…

"Do we know each other?" Wayne asked…

"We met in Target…"

"Oh yea… that's right… now I remember…"

"Mary?" Rhonda asked as she looked at me…

"Yes Rhonda – I'm pregnant!"

"Oh my God – I'm so happy for you – congratulations!" she said as she hugged me…

"What'd I miss?" Wayne laughed…

"Honey – that night we went shopping at Target – I got a pregnancy test – I wanted to surprise you – Rhonda let me cut in front of her to pay for it when you went to go get the car…

"Aww… that's sweet…" Raymond said as he pulled her into a kiss…

"What'd I miss?" I asked…

"I came in here looking for a living room set… Raymond asked me what he could get me… I said he could get me his number… he offered to take me to lunch… I told him I'd call him and let him know what time to pick me up to take me out to dinner…"

"And then she told me to make sure I help her pick out something comfortable because she needs her man to be comfortable when he comes over…" Raymond said as he kissed her again…

"Aww… that's beautiful…" Wayne said…

"So – which set did you end up with?" I asked…

"The same set you picked!" she answered as we all laughed.

Twisted Mary Tree

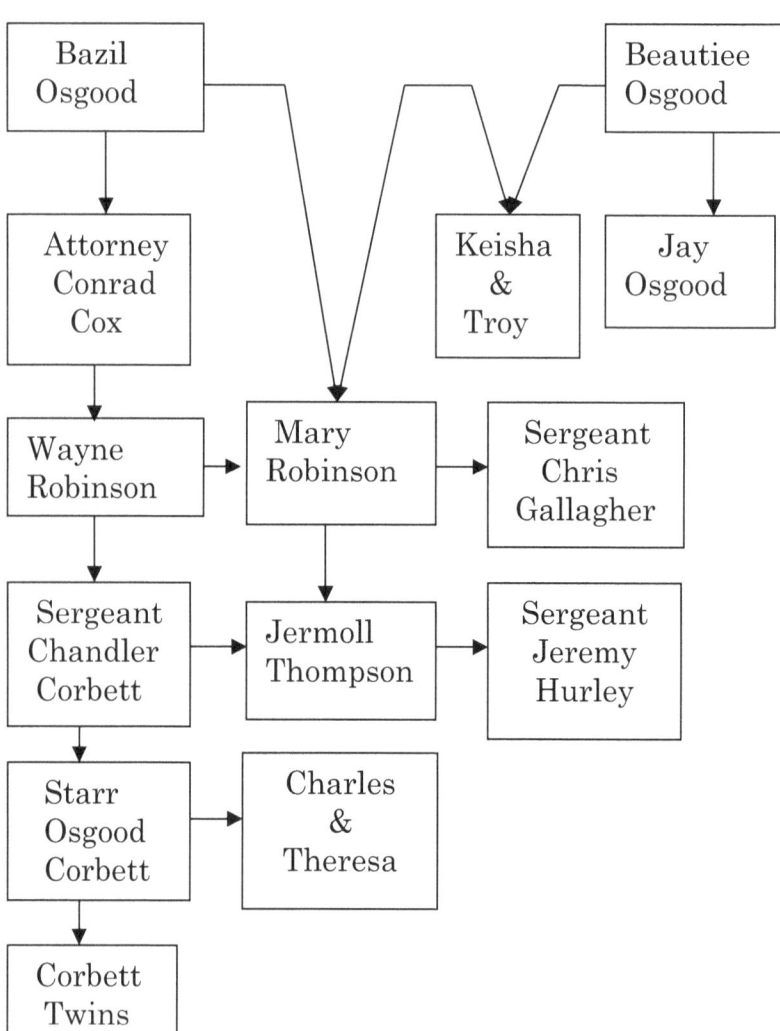